Dedications

Alizée, for the inspiration
All the members of Alizee-Forum.com
Lastly, My mom and sister Carolyn

And to that special someone…
You know who you are.

Book one: The Demon Within

Book two: In the Assassin's wake
(October 2007)

Book three: Project Moonlight
(October 2008)

Book design by: Dave Schofield
Cover model: Kayla Bryant
Photographer: Don Grogan
Edited by Carolyn Schofield

Published by Quentin Daschel Lee,
Fivi Daschel Odd Publishing Group.
4923 Calle Del Oya
Las Vegas, Nevada. 89120

First press edition: August 2006
ISBN-10: 0-9789007-0-7
ISBN-13: 978-0-9789007-0-0

Printed in the USA, LSI Print Press
Distributed by Fivi Daschel Odd Publishing group

10 9 8 7 6 5 4 3 2 1

Amelie could hear the screams. They echoed through the room with a resonating will. She was being assaulted by the torment carried in the voices. One of the men hit her and she felt the warm trickle of blood on her face. She started to go numb from the impact. Her face swollen, she passed out with the onslaught of pain wracking her mind.

The Demon Within

Quentin Daschel Lee

Prologue

"Motts…" The agent stated over the phone.

"Don't use my name again!" Motts replied. "What's the status of our project?"

"We are standing by waiting for your decision." Jones fidgeted over the phone and his voice was getting shaky. He stammered for an explanation but Motts interrupted him.

"Do you remember Project Moonlight?" Motts prodded.

"Yeah, but that was thirteen years ago…" Jones' voice lingered.

"I know… I want you to leak the file to our deep operatives in France…" Motts said at length.

Back then, Motts was a mission specialist and his only mission that failed was Project Moonlight. His record was almost spotless.

Director Motts was a tired looking man and he had a full head of hair with laces of gray streaks. Despite his efforts to hide them, the weary years were hard on Motts who was pushing fifty. Even though Motts was Director of the Central Intelligence Agency, he didn't look it.

"Do I make myself clear?" Motts' tone was growing defiant and he used this to his advantages when dealing with his agents.

"Yes sir, but might I ask about the status of the retired men?" Jones was getting more nervous by the minute and it showed in his voice.

"They are expendable." Motts stated. "The objective is to get her to resurface; I need you to start the process."

"Consider it done sir" Jones concluded.

Motts hung up the phone and his face transformed into a man of recollections. He pushed himself back to thirteen years ago when he'd first heard of the technology. Despite his efforts to obtain it, Motts considered the implications surrounding that operation. He'd sent operatives out to put themselves in a position to buy the technology but the scientist would not take the offer. At the time, he didn't know that the Russians were behind the funding that had been provided to the scientist and in lack of that information; Motts ordered a black ops team to steal it. The mission was a failure that ended in the deaths of a French couple and left the young girl orphaned. Then she had disappeared off the grid shortly after escaping an orphanage.

That was the last time he would hear of the case. Motts wondered what that little girl was doing now, wondered if she remembered anything from that fateful night.

Thirteen years had passed and out of nowhere, his intelligence operatives in Europe were reporting that spooks were inquiring about CIA operations in France. His team couldn't get specifics as to whom these spooks belonged to, or anything definitive about the information they were looking for, but it seemed to him that it was a sweep. Someone was following up on something that had happened in the past. He thought that it might have been the Russians again, but all had been quiet for the past few years. He hadn't heard a peep from any of his contacts in Moscow. It had to be someone else, but who?

His mind reeled at the thought of the little girl looking for answers. He imagined how the events would unfold; this was a second chance and so he ordered his new covert intelligence team to leak information about Project Moonlight. All he could do was hope that she took the bait. He would have agents ready to pick her up if she surfaced.

It was turning out to be a good day for Motts and he liked the idea of cleaning up the mess he left back in France thirteen years ago.

Yes, it was going to be a good day.

* * *

Amelie was playing down in the basement when she heard the noise. It frightened her and she was beginning to worry. She put her toys down and cautiously walked over to the stairs that led to the rest of the house. There was shouting in a language that she did not understand. She heard her mother's shrill scream. The sound chilled her to the bone and before she realized what she was doing, Amelie rushed up the stairs and bursting through the door.

It was dark inside and all of the lights were out. She could hear heavy footsteps, and she heard her dad talking, no it was more like pleading—she thought. She could tell that he was scared. She rushed into the kitchen were the source of the commotion came from and was met by a man. He turned to her and hit her with something. The impact sent her sprawling backward.

Amelie fell to the ground with a thud and half unconscious. She could still hear the commotion. She could still hear her dad yelling, a loud bang, and then her mother screaming. Somehow, Amelie was able to hear everything, the torment in her father's voice, the beating of her mother and the feeling of helplessness that engulfed her sub consciousness.

* * *

Amelie woke up, she was soaked from sweat and she had a slight fever. The wet sheets clung to her bare form and it made the chore of getting out of bed all the more difficult. She sat up and looked around the room, half-aware and half still asleep. She was looking for those men, but she knew that they would not be there and she knew that the events in her dream happened thirteen years ago.

Amelie stared into nothingness and her face began to contort. Tears started to well up in her eyes and she began to pout again. She curled up into a ball and tried to cry herself back to sleep. It never happened though and she decided to pull herself together.

She swallowed her sorrow down and started to think about what she wanted to do to the men that took her parents. The thought of vengeance seemed to give her a sense of stability and she started to turn her pain into hatred.

She climbed out of bed and pulled the sticky sheets from her well-defined body. The sweat that coated her form glistened in the moonlight from the window. She walked over to the bathroom and turned on the light. She rubbed her head trying to wash away her grogginess.

Amelie went over to the sink and fumbled with the water knobs. The running water from the faucet seemed to calm her and she bent low to splash herself with the warm water that she gathered in her hands. She repeated the action a few more times then looked into the mirror.

The woman that stared back at her was beautiful by all standards. She had straight long black hair, her thick yet definitive eyebrows were evenly groomed and they accented her bold green eyes. Despite the reddening around her eyes, her skin was soft and smooth. Hardly any blemishes scarred her face. Her full lips gave way to a distinctive jaw line that ended in small, well-shaped ears.

Amelie just stared into the mirror. She didn't see a young woman of barely twenty years, but instead a little seven-year-old girl who was frightened, sad, and lonely. She thought to herself that she was weak and she needed to turn that little girl into a monster. She wanted revenge for her parents' death. Wanted to make these men pay for the wrong they imposed upon her.

Not much occupied this room, save for a few towels, her bathrobe, some hygiene products, and a USP Tactical. She donned the robe and walked back into the apartment, grabbed her smokes and opened the sliding glass door. She was here on business and needed to be ready if anything were to happen. She picked up the phone and dialed a number.

* * *

It was morning when Amelie stepped into the foreign world of America. It was nothing like southern France where she grew up. There were buildings stretching into the sky and cars packed into the streets. This was New York; a place where one could easily make new friends. Moreover, she was here to make new friends.

Amelie always dreamt of being a dancer or singer, she never thought that she would end up looking for someone that claimed to have information on the death of her parents. She never thought that she would live a life of a criminal, learning the ins and outs of a secret underground world where enemies can become allies.

Throughout her childhood, Amelie ran with the toughest of criminals. From the streets of Paris where she escaped from the malicious grasp of an orphanage ran by a bitter and cruel woman, to the outskirts of France stealing valuable objects for associates.

Amelie had a mission and she did everything she could to learn the ways of combat, stealth, and observation. She lived a unique lifestyle that conditioned her; no, it was a way of thinking that ensured her survival. She didn't choose this way of life for a career, but as a tool to fight the demons that visited her in the night.

Amelie had met up with mercenaries, done some jobs with them and even seen the reality of crime at a tender age of thirteen. She killed a man once; he was forcing himself upon her and in her desperation, had stabbed him over twenty times. She never thought that the road that was paved before her would put her in a position to buy information on her parents' killers. She was lost in a world of hate and revenge.

She went to the place where she was told to contact a man who would help her in finding the murders. It was a dingy place on Manhattan's north side. It wasn't hard to find and she cautiously approached the building looking for signs of danger. It was still early in the morning and Amelie didn't trust anyone. She had been informed that the man she was to meet is a shady and dangerous person not to be underestimated.

Everything looked good but that wasn't any more comforting to her.

Amelie walked along the street towards her rendezvous point. People were rising for their daily routines and she hurried along the boulevard eager to get this business done. After fifteen minutes of walking, Amelie finally reached the location where she was instructed to wait.

* * *

She was definitely beautiful, almost more beautiful than his contacts in France had described. Tony watched her with a cautious eye. She seemed to be harmless but he knew from learning about her background that she was a dangerous woman. To Tony, all women were dangerous. Still though he measured her up to be a good acquaintance, someone he would want on his side if ever they were in the thick. Her reputation preceded her and when he had inquired about this strange French woman, he found out that she could be ruthless if driven hard enough.

He was in a unique position where information came to him easily and when he had gotten word that she was looking for information concerning the death of her parents, he planned his best to be on her receiving end. She was rich and price to her was nothing. This prospect was motivation enough to risk his profession.

Tony approached the woman and gave her a quick nod. He dropped an envelope with her name on it. He knew that she would wait a few moments to pick it up, knew that she would follow the instructions on the paper exactly. She was a professional and he knew that she was the type of person that took pride in that.

* * *

Amelie watched as a man moved toward her, she instinctively clutched the USP she brought with her. He was a rather tall man peaking over six feet yet he carried him self well. She knew that he was street smart; she knew that he was someone not to be toyed with.

His clothing was clean yet wrinkled. He wore a black jacket that had some logo on the back. His jeans were worn but lacking holes. His hair was short, cut in a flattop and it was a stark white. Amelie thought that he was grey, or he died it that color, she liked the look but warned herself that this man was just as dangerous has she.

As he approached, he gave a quick nod and dropped an envelope. She looked down and it had her name on it. She watched him walk down the street and then disappear into an ally before she picked it up. She hesitated a moment and realized the she was not wearing her gloves. She decided that it would be wise not to get her fingerprints on the paper if things went south. She put on her favorite gloves, picked up the paper, and walked across the street.

* * *

The door to her rented apartment was ajar and Amelie was beginning to wonder if she had been setup. She pulled out her USP and hid it in her jacket. She could hear commotion coming from within her room and slightly pushed the door open.

When she went in, she was instantly relieved to find the house cleaner was in there making her bed and cleaning up the place. She had forgotten about these kinds of services. Amelie relaxed and put the gun away.

When the housekeeper was done, Amelie tipped her some money, closed and locked the door. She did a once through the room, kitchen and bathroom to ensure nothing was missing or discovered. Everything looked good to her and she sat on the bed to open the envelope.

It was a list. There were twelve names on the list. Amelie was almost sure that these were the men she wanted dead. Two of the names had lines through them and there was a note on the bottom. It read:

Two of the entries were killed in combat. With their deaths verified, that would leave ten.

Amelie was pleased that some of her work had already been done and so she started to pack immediately. She had a long flight back to France and wanted to get a head start on locating these ten people.

* * *

"Is it done?" The man asked.

"Yes, she has the information and I think she will do well in completing her tasks." Tony said.

"Good, your compensation will be available in a few hours." The man stated. "I want you to keep an eye on her while she is here, ok?"

"Sure Mr. Motts, anything you say." Tony finished.

He hung up the payphone and moved back to the ally where he had walked through. He went back to the meeting place where he dropped the paper. He wanted to be sure that the woman he had seen was in fact the same woman he was told to monitor. The envelope was gone, and he was almost convinced that it was the right person. He checked the closest trashcans for good measure and didn't find any signs of his envelope.

It was her. All he needed to do was keep an eye on the incoming flights at Boston, New York, and New Jersey in the future, note her movements and report to Motts when things were cool.

The work was not bad for a few million bucks—he thought, and he didn't have to kill anyone.

* * *

Amelie was on the plane and in the air when she finally truly relaxed. She was jumpy all week while in New York and she was glad to be heading back home. It was an eight-hour flight from JFK to Paris and she took advantage of that time to sleep. Aside from being too exhausted to dream on those occasions where she had passed out, sleeping on planes seemed to allow her a moment of peaceful rest.

Then there were those days when the planes would experience turbulence and she would end up getting extremely sick. Nevertheless, the weather report mentioned that it would be a calm flight. Before she realized anything further, she was fast asleep.

Hours later Amelie was awakened by the captain of the plane over the intercom, he said that their arrival in Paris was just under an hour out. It was almost morning time and she was anxious to get back on the ground.

Amelie thought about all of the things she needed to do to be prepared for her tasks. She wanted get this part of her life over with and allow her parents the luxury of knowing that their killers were found and punished.

* * *

Just before nightfall, Amelie reached her home just outside Beuvron-en-Auge. The small town was about a kilometer from Marseille. She pulled into the garage and closed the door. The house looked as if it never had any inhabitants. She rarely came here and now that things were beginning to move, she would base all of her operations out of this little farm.

It was given to her through inheritance and she spent some summers here as a child. This place was full of good memories and she was glad to have received it.

Her parents mostly lived in Ajaccio, on the island of Corsica. That's where the tragedy that shaped her life happened. She would never go back there. After the funeral, she had the house emptied and boarded up. Most of the things were brought here and put into the basement. Amelie meant to go through everything, donate the items she didn't need and pack up the items that she wanted to keep. That never happened though and she was never around to tend to matters at hand.

When she decided to move to the little chateau, she spend the better part of a year, cleaning and restoring the home to par with its original 1781 year of construction. She learned about growing fruits and vegetables and planted some of her favorite foods.

Strawberries were one of her favorites and she had to learn all about caring for the bushes. She hired some farmers to do more of the heavier work around the farm. She never intended to commercialize the crops so they eventually got things into shape for her and her housekeeper to maintain.

Sandrine, her housekeeper was one of the sweetest women Amelie had ever known. Amelie offered her the job of keeping the place clean while she was away. As her trust fund stipulated that she could employ people to tend to responsibilities, she was not allowed to withdrawal money for personal use until her eighteenth birthday. Therefore, when Sandrine offered to pay Amelie some money each month in exchange for a bloated salary, she didn't hesitate to do so.

After Sandrine had passed away, Amelie moved into an apartment in Nice to square away all of her plans. They were in motion now and all she needed was to find these men and deliver justice for their crimes against her family.

It was a long a difficult road for her to travel, but Amelie was resilient and she possessed the motivation to drive her relentlessly.

She turned on her computer and waited for the operating system to load. She was knowledgeable with a computer as her dad specialized in the field. She had learned how to use computers at a young age, her understanding of how to use the internet for gathering information she needed came later.

She met up and dated a computer hacker from Sweden a few years back and she paid attention to everything he'd taught her. She was a resourceful person and knew how to get around in computer systems that she had broken into.

Now that she had the names of these men, she would run what the Americans called a credit report. Since all of them were retired from the CIA, she could easily get non-essential information on them from the reporting agencies. It would cost her some money to order the reports, but to her, money was not an issue. It was the names.

The reports came through in a series of emails and she printed each one off as they came in. She carefully plotted out her trips and dates with each target and she built an alias for moving in and out of the US.

Poised as a foreign exchange student, she would travel under that guise and secretly conduct the hits she planned. Amelie got maps of towns where these people lived in. She pulled up blueprints of buildings where they worked, stayed, and visited frequently.

Amelie spent the better part of two weeks gathering information, plotting her movements, and setting up locations for safe houses. She was ironing out every little detail, covering every little aspect of her tasks, angles and outcomes so that she could get in, kill and get out.

She was focused, refined and conditioned to operate like a machine. Her thoughts were bent on the sole promise that she would exact the justice that was long over due.

Chapter 1: No return

She never thought it would feel like this. She had taken a life before but that was a justified action. She was defending herself. Never had she murdered someone. No, she didn't murder anyone. She merely carried out the appropriate punishment for what he did to her parents so long ago. She carried the sentence for him until his day of reckoning.

Amelie sat in the alley clutching her Glock 23 in the rain. Her long black hair was stringy and matted with blood from a wound on the side of her head. It didn't go as planned and she was starting to doubt the success she envisioned. The rain was coming down hard and she needed to find a place to dry off.

Grabbing the prone man's wrist, she waited for him to jump and attack but that never happened. She checked his pulse to confirm that he was dead. It all happened too fast, she was not anticipating his reaction and he almost got the best of her. She managed to get a hold of her pistol and shoot him but not before, he slammed her on the side of the head with his phone. The blow sent her flying and to her luck, right where her gun landed.

He had fallen out the window from the gunshot. She imagined that the fall killed him and not the bullet. Three stories down, and she could see that his prone form was broken. She had run down the stairs to the alley as fast as she could to make sure that he was dead. It was late and in this part of town, there weren't many pedestrians about. She sat down and started to cry, she was shaking violently and the effects of her adrenaline rush were wearing off.

After a few long moments, she got up and composed herself then started back to the man's apartment. She needed to clean up after herself.

* * *

"Echo six bravo to control" Officer McReady said into the microphone.

"This is control, Echo six bravo, go head...," the woman at the other end prompted.

"I need you to expedite a paramedic to 5th and Michigan Ave. I've got an 804.

"Roger that Six Bravo, that's an 804." The female voice repeated.

Officer McReady was a beat cop. Pushing fifty, the man was a seasoned officer of Chicago PD. He was always neat and proper. His chiseled jaw gave him a distinct look and his thick eyebrows accented his forehead completing his stern look. The man was well known for his bust record and many of the other officers gave him the respect he commanded through the tone in his voice and the way he carried himself.

McReady put down the walkie-talkie and waited for homicide. However, his cop's intuition was kicking in and he thought about actually walking around to see if he could find something more. He shook his head and started to secure the crime scene. While deploying the police tape, he noticed that the man had a wound of some king in his belly. Further investigation revealed that the man was shot in the stomach. At first, he thought that the man was a suicide but it appeared that he'd been wrong.

The officer ran into the apartment building and up to third floor to find the room to the window. The door was kicked in. *Forced entry... shit!* He drew his gun and radioed for back up. McReady waited in silence and didn't know if the shooter was in the apartment or not, just that this was a murder and he might be in danger.

The cop couldn't hear a thing and the silence was like a jackhammer to his ears. Just then, the door on the other side of the hall opened.

* * *

Amelie was done packing and she left everything in her room neat and tidy. She was always well organized and clean. She had two more people to hit before returning to France and wanted to be done with it. Her first kill was a dramatic experience and all she could do to push through was to remember that these men murdered and raped her mother and shot her father.

In a false sense of achievement, it felt morbidly good to deliver vengeance to him. She didn't marvel in the act, but found the slightest bit of peace from the action. It surprised her just a little but Amelie knew that it was temporary; she knew that the dreams would come again and soon.

She absently opened the door to her apartment and suddenly she froze. There was a cop right in front of her. It took only but a second to register that he was not there for her but for the man across the hall. She had rented the apartment six days ago just so that she could study him, calculate and evaluate his awareness. It turned out to be a nerve-wracking experience and she was glad that it was all over.

The officer waved her back inside and all she could do was comply. She silently cursed herself for not leaving sooner. She had an appointment to make and this would cause her to miss her next target.

Amelie had planned to conduct a triple hit this weekend; two lived in the same city and the third in New York. She had carefully planned for each hit, how she would get away and what safe house to choose incase of discovery from the local authorities.

They were a joke. It was so easy to slip into the US under a false identity and execute missions with ease. Once she got into the borders, the domestic security could easily be bypassed.

She scanned the hallway before closing the door. It looked as if he were alone. Her window of opportunity would soon close when more cops would arrive. She put her stuff down and grabbed the Glock and a dagger. Scanning the room, she stuffed the two weapons under her shirt and went to the window.

Sure enough, there was only one squad car in the street. She could see the side of the car from her angle and she continued to scan the area for more cops. She estimated that she had about another two minutes before the place would be crawling with them. She thought about holding out but she didn't want to stay in the same place for too long. Besides her lease on the apartment was up in a few hours and she didn't want to be around when the detectives come knocking. She put her non-essential belongings next to the front door and opened the window.

Amelie made her way to the hospital and along the way; she looked for a good place to dispose of the Glock she used on her first victim. There was a trash truck crew running their rounds down a side alley. She waited for the moment when they would climb back into the truck and go to the next stop.

She watched and when the time had come, she ran up to the truck and tossed the weapon in.

* * *

The evening air was crisp for a night in Chicago and the bustle of nightlife activities at Chicago Hope Hospital was in full motion. Nurses and doctors milled about tending to the sick and injured. Amelie was walking through the halls pretending to be lost. She was in the Trauma ward where people were taken with life threatening injuries. She wasn't there visiting anyone but rather, she was looking for a doctor. Her head was aching. She used the injury as a cover to get closer to her next victim. He was a medical surgeon at this hospital.

Earlier that week she had flown in from New York where she watched her third target. She would execute her hit on him after these two. The first was a helicopter pilot who proved an almost easy target. In hindsight, she figured that she could have done a more clean job, but it was her first and she had only done it once before.

Still though, taking someone's life was always nerve wracking.

A nurse grabbed her as she was walking down the hall. The icepack that Amelie was pressing on her head almost slipped from her grasp.

"Excuse me, ma'am, but you can't be back here." She stated flatly.

"I'm headed to treatment." Amelie explained. Her accent caught the nurse off guard and she straightened herself and looked at Amelie's wound.

"It doesn't look that bad miss, who is your doctor anyways?" The nurse gave Amelie a questioning look.

"I forget his name, but he is waiting for me in the room, I had to use the laboratory." Amelie shrugged.

"Well you better get going before security comes along and escorts you out." She paused. "You'll have to wait another hour before you get treatment."

Amelie nodded and continued to walk down the hall to the man she would soon kill.

He wasn't an attractive man but his physique was still clearly seen under his smock. He had broad shoulders and well defined biceps. Amelie knew that this person could easily handle her if she gotten into a melee with him. She would take special care to ensure that it would never happen. The doctor was balding for a man in his late thirties and his hair, while still dark, was showing signs of gray. He still wore his military issue subscription glasses that seemed to hang on his hawkish nose.

Amelie reached into her handbag and placed her hand on the dagger that was hidden inside and she entered the room. As she entered, she closed the door behind her. The man looked up at her, smiled and adjusted his glasses.

"Can I help you ma'am?" the doctor said.

"Yes..." Amelie defiantly stated. "You are going to look at the cut on my forehead?"

"What is your name dear?" he asked politely. The man turned around to grab the paperwork on the table.

Amelie pulled out the dagger and rushed in. The blow was solid and it hit him in the lower spine. The man jerked back and Amelie had to lean into him to keep herself steady. He started to groan loudly and she covered his mouth with her other hand while pushing against his weight with her shoulder. He struggled but it was no use... the paralyzing blow was enough to rob him of his strength. It was almost perfect. She thought of how easy it would have been with her gun, but it would have been too noisy. Besides, she'd already disposed of it earlier. Her instincts were to be quick and silent, and so she was exactly as her instincts predicted

Blood spilled to the floor and a puddle was fast forming. She surmised that she had hit the spot that was intended. The wicked blade was long enough to puncture his kidney and the color of the blood was a deep red signifying just that. He weakly kicked out trying to push her off, but it was no use.

"Be still, let it happen." She whispered to him. "Do you remember me?"

"Yes I think you do… thirteen years ago in France, my love."

He half turned to her with a look of horror. His face looked pale and his eyes were dark. She kissed him on the cheek and allowed him to slide to the floor over the puddle at her feet.

His protest soon ended when the last bit of life left his body. She released the dagger and left it in his body as a mark that she had come. Amelie stood up mindful of the blood that was under his body and carefully stepped back.

Amelie looked around for anything that would serve as a cleaning agent. She needed to secure the room, clean out her presence and make her get away. That went well, really well. Amelie was pleased that he didn't put up a fight. Then again, he didn't get a chance to. Her wicked smile seemed to provide little comfort to her and Amelie though about the final thoughts of recognition he might have had toward her.

It didn't matter though; his death was not for his benefit but more for hers' and her parents. She felt strange, almost as if she had sympathy for the form lying at her feet. The moment grew awkward and that notion brought her back from her lingering thoughts.

Amelie had to leave before this man starts to miss his appointments. There were more that needed to be taken care of and she intended to complete her vendetta. It was a kind of bittersweet taste, interestingly enough though she found that the next few months would prove to be the most important in her life. Amelie's seriousness was only fractured by time. Her time in France would prove to be the most important. She could plot and plan out her hits with confidence and anonymity. Right now, she had to get back to New York, she had unfinished business there.

* * *

The commotion on the street was enough to keep Amelie away from her apartment. Her flight back to New York was leaving soon and her deadline to checkout was narrowing fast. She needed to get into her room and collect her things.

The police had the area sealed off from pedestrians and residents. They were meagerly wandering about the street chatting with each other as if it was just another night on the force. This was surprising to her and she became somewhat amused at the sight. This was Chicago's police force hard at pretending to work and they weren't really working at all.

Amelie peered at the entrance to her building, there were cops moving in and out of the area and she thought for a moment that she would never get in. Just then, one of the tenants started to argue with a cop. She was complaining that they would not allow her in because of her color. Amelie viewed this moment as a potential break and she moved closer to the entrance while trying not to attract the attention of the officers.

She was standing next to the door when the woman became violent. The officer closest to her rushed over to help his partner. She slipped in and immediately ran up the back stairs to her room. When she reached the third floor, she was greeted by a young and hansom officer. She smiled at him and the man nodded his approval. She walked past and eventually made it to her room. She could hear the detectives in the other room talking about the crime.

She could hear over their radios that someone had stabbed an employee at the hospital and that there were no eyewitnesses or suspects.

Amelie was relieved to hear that news. It meant that she had done what she intended to do without problems. She opened the door to her room and gathered up her bag, smiled at the cop at the door across the way and started to walk out.

"Ma'am?" the officer said.

"Yes?" Amelie responded.

"Excuse me, but you can't leave. This is a crime scene and we need to interview you." The cop continued.

"I know, this stuff isn't mine, it's my sisters'... Your detective wants to talk with me down stairs." She confessed.

Her heart was racing, she had just killed two people and now this cop was putting a huge obstacle in her way.

"Ok ma'am, as long as you are aware." He concluded.

Amelie smiled and walked off. She went down the stairs to the second floor where there were hardly any cops at all. She waited for the last of them to go back up on the other side of the complex then she moved down the hall to the window that overlooked the roof of the building next to the complex.

Her escape was preplanned and she checked the route before she even entered the building. All was clear for her to walk out of the crime zone and to the airport.

* * *

He was a sorry sap of a man and his mental condition worsened everyday. The frail man that served in the military for twenty years before working for some secret group in the government wasn't much to look at. He was aging over forty, but anyone looking at him would think he'd been ten years younger. He was a soldier that's for sure. The tattoos that decorated his arms and chest were ornamented with the traditional *semper fi* logos.

Lynn Li was the nurse that was in charge of caring for the invalid. Something had happened to him on a mission years ago and his next of kin dropped him off here and never came back. She always wondered about him and his background. What did he do for the government? Why would they just dump him in some rundown ragged nursing home on the out skirts of New York?

Lynn was a Korean girl who came over seas years ago and her definitive features were often mistaken for Chinese or of the Philippines. She was beautiful by those standards and her soft smooth skin belied her true age. Her ever-observant eyes always darted back and forth with curiosity and she always seemed interested in who ever she talked with.

She was short and petit. Like any typical Asian, yet her beauty always seemed to shine through. Her long black her that she often wore in a bun, was like silk floating on the surface of a bed of cream that was her back. This girl was well shaped and her tight shirt struggled to hide the contours of her ribbed stomach. She wore a sports bra underneath her shirt that failed to compress her large breasts that were topped with pointy nipples.

This man had visitors once; three men dressed in black suits came in and tried to speak with him. Lynn was not allowed to talk with the men, but she did over hear a conversation they had with the general manager. She assumed from what she had heard that these men were government as well.

That was long ago. Lynn possessed a level of empathy for this particular person. Normal people cared for their sick kin but this man's family was nothing normal. They would pay the bills, yet never even requesting any information about his condition or progress. It was as if they didn't even care about him. Lynn was sad about that and felt for the poor guy.

She finished getting him into bed for the evening and put away the dirty sheets she'd pulled off earlier. She was about done for the day and wanted to get out before her sadness became too much. It always depressed her when dealing with this guy and she dreaded being in the room for too long. Still though, she cared for him as if he were her brother and provided to him a level of love that he'd been neglected.

Often times she would talk to him about her relationship problems. He never responded of coarse and she knew why. He was practically brain dead and yet still offered the shoulder of a quiet listener.

She finished up and turned out the lights, closed the door and leaned against it. She tried to brush away her sadness and compose herself a little. However, it was difficult

* * *

Amelie waited patiently as the nurse finished her chores and putting her target down for the night. She could see the empathy that this nurse had for the man and almost regretted the decision to kill him. She thought about sparing him the convenient death and allowed him to live in his private little hell. Then again, if he were mentally disabled then he probably would never feel the guilt of what he did to her parents.

As soon as the nurse closed the door, Amelie started to work on the window's lock. It wasn't hard because of the gaps in the window's seal were large enough to fit her tools. Soon, she would unlock the window's latch and slide it open. Death would come into that room and it would deliver its justice to the evil that lay helpless on the bed.

Amelie heard the grounds' security from around the corner. She quickly jumped down from the window's ledge and into the bushes. The men walked on obliviously chatting away about some crazy night in some sleazy strip club they've experienced together. Amelie hated American men, they were pigs and she could never see herself with any of them.

After the men passed she got back up on her perch and instantly realized that the men seen her. They came around the building again with their flashlights shining on her brightly.

Amelie calmly jumped down and came out of the bushes. They raised their batons and moved in to flank her.

"Well, well, what do we have here?" The first one stated as more of a taunt than a question. He wore a smile of ecstasy on his face and Amelie despised that look.

"Looks like we found a bit of fun to me Alex" the second one said to the other.

"We can have some fun tonight, Peter" Alex replied.

"I think you boys found more than you can deal with... be smart and walk, forget you've ever seen me..." Amelie spoke.

Alex half laughed while Peter stopped short with a curious look of interest on his face.

Amelie knew he was reacting to her French accent. It was a bit amusing and Amelie winked at the man out of seriousness.

"I think we should to take her into one of the vacant rooms, what do you think Pete?" He stated with a devious smile.

"Last chance..." was all Amelie said in return.

At that moment, Alex moved in slowly and Amelie half watched him get closer while keeping an eye on Pete. She produced a long black dagger from her sleeve and it slid into her hand with ease. She reversed her grip on the blade and hid it behind her forearm.

Alex came closer and tried to grab Amelie's arm. Big mistake... with blinding speed Amelie kicked the man in the gut and he doubled over and fell on his butt. Peter raised his baton and took a swing at the Amelie. It was high and she easily sidestepped into his swing. She spun around and struck at the man's neck with a quick slice as he passed. Instead of following the passing Pete, she reversed her turn to face Alex who was getting up.

Pete fell to his knees and found it hard to breathe. His neck was spewing blood from a four-inch gash from his jugular to his Adam's apple. Alex watched as his friend slumped to the ground twitching and then not moving at all.

He was horrified and somewhat paralyzed. She came in then and he raised his baton in defense but everything seemed to move too slowly for him. She was fast, faster than he was and before he could react, she was pushing that wicked blade into his throat. Their eyes connected for a brief moment. It was like a dance of death and Alex truly realized the beauty that was Amelie. He pleaded to her in his last moments of consciousness for forgiveness and she responded with a kiss on his mouth.

* * *

After dragging the two bodies out of sight, Amelie finished her business on the window and entered the room where her third target slept. She examined the room and listened for any signs of visitors. All was quiet and she felt confident that she could finally get to work.

She moved over to the bed and raised the bloody blade over the form. Then she paused a moment. The blood dripping from the knife made a quiet thudding sound as it hit the sheets. Amelie wanted him to be awake before she delivered her justice. She looked around for something that she could use to gag him. In the bin, there were dirty socks and Amelie reached in and grabbed a couple.

With the gag in his mouth, Amelie slapped him into consciousness. He responded with wide eyes. Yet there was no intelligence behind them. It almost unnerved her but she made a vow and planned to keep it. She slid the knife into his left ventricle and watched as he started to scream. It wasn't loud because of the gag, but he reached up and pulled it off.

"Merde" she fretted.

How could she be so stupid, just because he was an invalid that didn't mean he didn't have functional motor skills. The commotions behind the door caused an alarm in Amelie.

* * *

The door swung open and Lynn Li rushed in not understanding the moment's situation. She stopped suddenly and realized that the man she cared for all those years was dying from a wound on his neck.

Before she could react, her eyes were locked into a dance with the killer's gaze. A look of shock mirrored each other and Lynn could feel the terror sinking in. Those eyes seemed to calm her a little and she started to become lost within them. Her soft, green eyes were mesmerizing and they possessed a level of definitive commitment like none other. Mysterious and enchanting, they seemed to burrow down to Lynn's soul making her feel naked. The girl reacted first and grabbed Lynn by the shoulders. Her grasp was strong and controlling and Lynn found that all she could do was comply.

The girl pulled Lynn closer, so close that their noses almost touched. Then she did something to Lynn that she'd never have expected. The assassin pursed her lips. Like the girl was calming a frightened child. Lynn could hear the soft whisper of this Assassin breath blow up against her mouth. Her lips quivered for a moment and Lynn felt those eyes communicating to her. Talking with her, telling her that everything would be ok. Yet the girl did not speak.

The girl softly pulled Lynn's gaze to the floor and let her go. When Lynn dared to look up she was gone and the only thing that marked her passing was the black dagger that protruded from the neck of her patient.

* * *

"He's dead... along with two others. I fear that any one of us would be next..." The voice said over the phone.

"Who..." John asked.

"The doc, Jacob Malby and Henry Thoms where killed last week." The voice said. "And Richards was killed a few days ago."

"Yeah but wasn't Richards already dead? I mean he was pretty much comatose." John pried.

"That's right... and they were all ex CIA, on our team. Someone is hitting us... be on the look out." The voice warned. "And what ever you do... this stays off the books..."

The man hung up and left John to his recollections. Memories of events past were circling through his mind. He was trying to figure out who would order these hits. One after another, John dated their actions, their missions and anything about a black dagger but he could not remember beyond a few years. That was the signature of the killer, a black dagger. Well almost, Thoms was killed with a .40 cal round and two others were killed with the exact same knife.

That knife, there was something to it—he thought, but what? John turned off the light and pulled the covers over his shoulder. He had a lot to think about and tomorrow was no better.

* * *

The reports spelled out a death trail over the past few days and John was secretly inquiring of the status of the case. After his phone call, he started to monitor this killer's movements and any other relevant information on the case. He wasn't in charge of the cases in Chicago, but the one in his city was his to investigate. Once he'd seen the murder weapon, he knew instantly who was behind the killings. However, he had nothing except for the description of a seven year old and the link between Ted, his partner and the knife.

Chapter 2: The Hunter

She walked along the sidewalk, stalking her prey. He was a man in his mid thirties and going bald. What hair he did have was a sandy blonde color. His dark suit was well pressed and she fretted having to ruin it. Not overly fit for an older man, standing roughly six foot even, he looked rather pathetic to most. However, she knew his skills, knew what he was capable of doing.

She watched him closely, gauging his movements, calculating his reflexes. He was looking for someone, she knew, and she would make sure that he never found the person he was looking for. Unsuspecting pedestrians walked past her from both directions. They seemed to walk in slow motion as her gaze was fixed on to him, waiting for the right moment.

She was masterful at deception; the thought of anyone getting the better of her was beyond her imagination. The police could never figure out who she was and they were always three steps behind, except this one. He was also one of the force's best homicide detectives.

She had killed three of her ten targets in his own back yard and he was slowly catching on. This man had followed her movements through a trail of dead bodies and he even had a false description of her but why take him here, why now? He was the closest person ever to figure out who she really was. He wouldn't tell anyone though; being tied to her would spell forty years in prison. Cops in prison usually never survived past their first year. Either way, it was a death sentence.

She envisioned how the encounter would play out. She could see it in her mind, every detail to the confrontation. Every little thing she needed to accomplish before she was even close enough. She started towards him weaving in and out of the people on the sidewalk. She approached him, then flanked. It was the corner where people gathered to cross. It was in the lunch hour and real estate for shoulder room was in short supply. She easily slipped past the pedestrians unnoticed. Her timing, disciplined and calculated as always, was perfect.

A commotion stirred his attention and he looked away from her, a street hoodlum had stolen a purse from a citizen and tried to run, but ran in to a patrol officer. He didn't get far. She had been waiting for this moment. She prepared herself for the strike.

* * *

Jonathan Lee turned into the most beautiful of women he'd ever seen. So captivated by her charming yet wicked smile, he didn't even register the hot sensation against his chest. It was warm feeling against the cold pale color of her face. As the blade slipped unnoticed through his ribcage, he felt the euphoria of beauty wash over him. It was her beauty and he welcomed it.

She was holding him steady, their eyes locked into a dance of sorrow and compassion. She smiled at him, kissed him on the lips, and then he felt pain. She shoved him away, and he became dizzy. Before he realized that his favorite white shirt had become wine red, she was gone. John looked back and forth. Someone screamed as he fell to his knees. *The woman... where is she? Will she come back?* These were the last thoughts racing through his mind before he slipped into the cold, empty darkness.

She walked away without even being seen, disappearing in to the sea of many people that lined the streets. Falling from her gloved hand was the glinting dull flash from a black dagger.

* * *

The detective arrived on the scene to assess the death of his partner. There was the usual yellow, do not cross tape surrounding his partner's form. Police were moving people away from the area and news crews were told to back away until later. Clicks and flashes of cameras brought the detective from his thoughts.

He wasn't sure why Lee's assassin would strike out in the middle of daylight, when the streets were bustling with hundreds of eye witnesses, either she became more careless in her vendetta against them or she was sending a message. He figured that the killer's intent was the latter... that had to be it.

When dealing with someone that has eluded the law for weeks, Barns would not put it past this dangerous assassin. Another officer came about to yield a knife in a bag labeled evidence. Sure enough it was a bloodstained dagger, and tests would yield that it was Lee's blood on the blade he was sure of it. Moreover, he was sure that the knife would not have any traces of the killer's DNA or prints. She was precise, thorough and clean. That scared Lee and he shared the same sentiments.

"I knew he was too close." the detective speculated. He spoke more to himself than to the officer.

"There wasn't anything else...," the other officer offered.

"Of course not... she is elusive to say the least." He stated quickly.

He knew who she was, or he had an idea of who she was. Nevertheless, he was in a position to keep things quiet. He was afraid that if someone found out the truth, he and his friends would be finished. Therefore, he continued the charade of not knowing who she was.

Detective Barns walked around and chatted with witnesses, but he didn't find any good leads. They all were too pre-absorbed in their own business even to notice someone being stabbed. How pathetic he thought. It occurred to him that he might better probe for information from a homeless bum.

He looked about and noticed a man half sleeping in the ally adjacent to where is partner now lay. The man smelled of putrid beer. Dirt caked his cheeks and the clothes he wore looked as if they were from some prehistoric cave of garbage. The long and matted beard he bore had flies clinging to crumbs of food that were decorating his mane like ornaments on a Christmas tree. The detective was not particularly interested in interviewing him here, so he decided to arrest the man for drunk in public charges. He was sure that it wouldn't be the first time.

He grabbed the closest patrol officer on the scene but instead found himself staring at the most beautiful girl he'd ever seen in is life. She looked surprisingly familiar. She was wearing a black trench coat with thigh high boots that barely met the short tight skirt that squeezed her waist. Her top was slim and barely cupped the woman's well-defined bosoms. Her hair was jet black and it flowed from her face rather smoothly in the wind.

She was standing tall despite her short stature. He could not turn away. He felt as if he did, the world would end. She slowly turned to him letting her eyes wander until she met his. Their gazes locked and he could feel himself warming up, felt his trousers move. She was a goddess. Her smile broke his mesmerized glare and it was instantly replaced by a look of stark embarrassment.

He turned to offer her some decency and when he turned back, she was gone. He rushed to the curb and looked up and down the street, but she was lost in a blanket of people covering the sidewalk. Barns wondered if he'd ever have the fortunes of seeing her again... probably not. His pessimism overruled any shred of hope stirring from his most recent fantasies. Still though, she looked familiar, as if he had seen her before, a long time ago perhaps. Enough playing around Barns, he thought... *I have to interview this witness.*

* * *

Barns went back to the scene were his partner lay. The secret that they held was coming back to haunt them and Barns still didn't know everything that Lee figured out. It was frustrating to say the least. What had been more frustrating was waiting for her to make her next move.

"Barns!" a man yelled. "Get your ass over here!"

Barns complied. He knew that the investigating detective would want to ask him questions and he knew that the story they cooked up once Lee found out more information was enough to sedate the Detective's curiosity. He just needed more time.

* * *

Later that day, Barns interviewed the bum and found that he had been sleeping for most of the day. A lot of good that did, just then his phone rang. Barns got a dreadful sensation at that moment. He thought that if he picked up the phone, he would run into more misery. Sure enough, the call was his wife. She had managed to track him down primarily to nag at him for not doing as she asked.

The other detectives knew this routine and merely felt sorry for the guy. They snickered at him for always replying... *yes dear,* and *I know dear*. This was usually followed by, *it won't happen again dear... I know... I mean it this time.* Anything to get her off the phone, but then, this time it was a little different.

"You have a package here for you, when are you coming to get it? Can you bring me some fresh tomatoes for supper? And while you are at it, pick up some milk... we are out of milk... are you there Ted? Oh... and we are out of dish soap."

Her tone was like a wind that would never end... All Ted Barns could say was, "I'm on it."

"Who is this package from Ted? Are you seeing someone? Its smells like a woman. You better not be cheating on me!" Ted hung up the phone.

It didn't even occur him until he was getting up to clock out for the day when he realized that he had a package that smelled like a woman in his wife's' hands. What was that all about? With haste, Ted gathered his briefcase and grabbed his keys, left the office and ran to his car. This was getting spooky and he needed to find out what was going on.

* * *

She watched him exit the police station. He was in a hurry and she thought that he'd gotten the news. Sure enough as she followed him, she already knew where he was headed. Men are so weak—she scoffed. With a hint of a smile creeping across her lips, she almost laughed. It was like a little school girl giggling at the boy in the sandbox. This wasn't going to be hard at all.

* * *

He went right home as expected. When he got in, he was immediately assaulted by a woman bearing curses and threats. He ignored them and demanded the package. His wife handed the rather large, somewhat heavy box to him. He carried it over to the living room and checked the label. It was addressed to him and the paper used was pink. Pink... how odd and it smelled of perfume.

He was curious and he thought that it was something that had been mixed up with someone else's mailbox that had his name. It wasn't uncommon these days to receive a package addressed to you by accident. The mail system sucked.

"Can you get my knife dear?" He insisted.

"What is it?" She replied.

"Get my knife!" he yelled. She cringed in response and moved over to the bedroom where he kept his 'toys' all the while mumbling to herself.

He looked outside and noticed an SUV parked across the street. One he'd never seen before. The windows were tinted dark as midnight. It was running he knew, the hot exhaust clashed with the cold winter air. It was spewing steam like a train. It was a cop's job to notice things unusual and he'd never seem it there before. His paranoia was getting to him so he thought he'd better check it out.

Barns moved to the door and before he opened it, he checked his firearm. It was loaded and he felt good about that. He holstered the Glock and opened the door. Barns immediately noticed that the SUV had no plates. Walking towards the truck didn't prove hard at all. However, Barns didn't want to alarm the occupant. He pretended to grab the morning paper that his wife always forgot the get for him. It was close enough to the street to put him in a better position.

The vehicle was clean, black and sleek. It said to him that '*I am pristine*' He thought of getting one himself. The wife would never go for it.

He bent down to grab the paper and... BOOM!!!!!!! He realized at that moment that he was floating, no; flying into the street. He had been thrown by a blast. He fell into a roll and looked back at his house only to see it in flames. Shattered glass littered the lawn and the street. He felt pain in his back. He could not hear anything because his eardrums were ringing. Broken wood and shingle started to fall to the ground. He leaned and rolled trying to get his balance. It was no use.

What the fuck happened he thought? His mind was racing... he had to get in there and save his wife. He watched as the door to the SUV opened and he could see soft smooth legs emerge from the darkness within. He watched as the black leather two-inch boot heels that adorned the smooth legs met the ground. She was graceful. His gaze started to follow up her body and when he got to the woman's face, he recognized her! He knew it! She was it, the assassin.

His mind went screaming for him to take action. He reached for his gun but found instead forlorn emptiness. She walked closer. He looked to his left and found the Glock lying in the street. It was out of reach.

He tried to get up, but he was assaulted by pain in his back. She came closer. He rolled over to see his attacker. It was the most magnificent thing he'd ever seen. Her beauty seemed to calm him. It was like a mother, settling a baby. She had an aura about her that engulfed him. He steadied his breath waiting for the killing blow, but it never fell. She just stood over him and watched. Her dark eyes piercing him, reading his thoughts, then she bent low to get closer to him and he didn't resist. She smelled so good. Her hair was long and black just as before. It brushed his arm and it made him tingle. She smiled at him and moved her hand to his cheek. The warmth of her touch was divine! She was maternal ecstasy and he found himself wanting more.

Who was this mysterious woman? The soft caress of her fingers penetrated his soul; it gave him something... peace. He felt peace. She was the harbinger of death and yet at the same time, his spiritual peacekeeper. He fell into darkness then. He could feel her there still and for some reason wasn't worried. All he could do was smile as he slipped away.

In the last moments of his thoughts, he felt her leave him. NOOOO! He wanted to scream! Nothing came out. He felt the coldness reaching into his soul, claiming it. He tried to resist but he didn't have the energy. Barns fell away into what he thought was hell, his peace taken from him, and the scent of god leaving his presence was more than he could bear. The betrayal was complete when Barns knew no more.

* * *

She stood up, leaving the knife in Barns' neck. She glanced around and noticed people peering at her. She looked to the gun on the ground and bent low to pick it up. The neighbor across the street was an older man in his late sixties, probably a good time for him—she thought. She moved as fast as lightning towards the man. He stood there frozen in time. Her graceful stride was matched only by her acute keen accuracy. Three rounds went off and the man, gasping for breath, moved his hand up to a tight group of holes in his chest. He tried to stop the blood from flowing freely but he didn't have the energy to continue the movement. He felt the air rushing past his face, watched as the ground slammed into him.

She dropped the pistol on the ground next to the fallen man and then glanced at the rest of the people watching her. They all started to move inside and as each one vanished from the outside world, she would stare at the next one until they were all gone. Satisfied that they got the message, she got in the Chevy Tahoe and sped off. That didn't go as well as she thought.

* * *

Amelie arrived in France later that week and was driving out to her estate when she came across a little girl on the side of the road. She was holding a lifeless dog. The girl was dressed in a thatched knitted dress. It was a bit dirty from prolonged use but the little girl didn't seem to mind. She looked to be around the age of ten, maybe twelve Amelie guessed.

Amelie stopped the car and got out. She walked over to the little girl on the road and bent down next to her. She immediately noticed that the girl was crying. The tears had washed away most of the dirt that was painted on her face.

"Hey there, you ok?" she whispered.

The girl just sat there holding the dead animal. Amelie looked at the dog and she could see that the beast had been hit by a car or truck. It was recent, she observed. The dog didn't develop that putrid smell yet.

"Honey, you can't be out in the street, you'll get hit like your dog did." She explained.

"Help me bury him, please?" The little girl said.

"Sure" was all Amelie could say.

* * *

Amelie finished burying the pup when the little girl said her final words to the dead dog. She had used stones to cover the animal since she didn't have a shovel available. Amelie noticed that she called the dog Susu. It was an odd name for a dog but Amelie didn't mind too much. She was more worried about the little girl's mental state.

She waited for the girl to finish and then offered her a ride home. They climbed into the car and she drove towards the closest town, which for her was in between them and her estate.

"So, little one, what is your name?" Amelie asked with a smile.

"Tryst" the girl replied. "Well, more like Trystine... but my friends call me Tryst for short."

"That is a pretty name for a pretty girl." Amelie complimented. "My name is Amelie. But you can call me Lili for short."

"Is that what your friends call you?" the girl prodded.

"I have no friends Trystine." She said somberly. "Do you want to be my friend?" she finished.

"We can be friends, but I have to warn you... you better not lie to me!" Trystine scolded. "I don't like it when people lie to me."

"I won't lie to you Tryst, I have no reason to." Amelie assured her.

They reached the edge of town and Tryst motioned for Amelie to stop. She climbed out of the car and waved a goodbye at Amelie.

"Hey, if you need anything, I live right up the hill on Lyon street" She hollered after the girl. "It's the only house on the hill!"

Trystine waved a goodbye in response to the offer. Amelie knew that she would see the little girl again soon. She watched as the girl ran down the street. It was late in the evening and Amelie wondered about that girl. She didn't know anything about her but just from looking at her. Amelie would guess that she was an orphan, or even homeless for that matter. She would have to do something about that some time.

Chapter 3: Morality

In the foggy memory of her dreams, Amelie could hear the screams. They echoed through the room with a resonating will. She was being assaulted by the torment carried in the voices. One of the men hit her and she felt the warm trickle of blood on her face. She started to go numb from the impact. Her face swollen, she passed out with the onslaught of pain wracking her mind.

Every night she had these dreams, they always woke her in a cold sweat. Completely dazed by the searing memory of her childhood, Amelie felt the tightening of her throat. Felt the pain from last night's dream well up within her. She put her head in her hands and began to weep and the tears flowed with out resistance. She would let it come. Welcoming it in its entirety, it was a ritual for her.

However painful it had been, she'd never forget what had happened so long ago. Some say that crying is a way of cleansing the soul. For her though, it was a constant reminder of dread that had followed her through the years.

Even though she was just twenty, it seemed that she had lived more than a hundred years compared to others. It wasn't always like this. Amelie forced happier thoughts of her life forward. She tried to grasp hope that one-day things would be better. That she can find the love that was stolen from her.

"Time to go to work again" she said aloud, more to herself than to the empty walls surrounding her existence.

She stood. Her bare form being accentuated by the yellow glare from the room's only window. Sweat was glistening off her back and neck. Gathering up a bathrobe, she put it on and walked into the kitchen where she would continue her morning ritual of coffee and a smoke. How she had fallen. Not even finishing the cigarette, or even putting it out for that matter, she walked back into her room and sat at a desk.

Not much else decorated the room, just a bed, her desk, a few pieces of luggage and an ammo box. In front of her on the wall just above the laptop she used, was news clipping and pictures of people. Military people from years ago, the age of the clippings and printouts were clearly marked on the headlines. Some of the pictures had 'exes' through them.

She picked up a marker and crossed out two more. There were only five more to go. Amelie powered up her computer and entered in a password. The computer started up and she opened a browser. A few quick searches revealed the location and maps of her next target. She wrote the directions down and pinned it to the wall next to the picture.

A little over two weeks had passed since her last visit to the states. She would have to plan and be more thorough this time. She was getting the idea that someone was catching on to her movements. Though they have not openly pursued her as the cops have, she was aware of them. She knew they had noticed her. It didn't matter, she was almost done and when it was all over she would find a small hole and crawl under it to escape the dreams.

She started to pack a lead lined box. It was large, large enough to fit a dismantled rifle inside. She then proceeded to close the box; she sealed it and attached a label to it. Stripping herself of the robe, she walked into the bathroom and turned on the shower. In a few minutes, the steam would fog up the window and mirror. Not a big deal, she wasn't concerned with looks, didn't even care about make up or any of the girly things most her age would trouble themselves with.

The water slid smoothly down her bare skin. It felt good to her and she always spent a few extra minutes in the shower than most. Sometimes she'd even run the hot water all the way out. She glanced over to the pistol in the shower. The trusty USP45, it was American made and hard to come by in France. Regardless it was a finely machined gun, very reliable and most importantly, it was loaded.

A knock at the door startled her. She never had visitors, and she grabbed the gun, not even bothering to cover herself up, she'd moved to the door and stood to the side of it, back against the wall. She cocked her ear toward the door and listened for anything that would give away her visitor. *Click,* she removed the safety from the gun.

"Hello Amelie, are you there?" She heard a little girl's voice question. She relaxed and replied "Hi... give me a minute."

Amelie moved to the bathroom, grabbed the robe, and put it on. This was going to be a good day.

* * *

After spending the previous day with Trystine who was just a tender and fragile age of twelve years old, the girl from the small town, Beuvron-en-Auge, a kilometer away that had befriended her. Amelie booked a flight to New York three weeks in advance. Her plan was to ship the rifle to an address she had reserved on an apartment in some small town in Massachusetts. She stopped for a minute to smile at Trystine. She and Tryst, as she liked to be called, had spent the day talking and laughing at stupid jokes while picking strawberries in the countryside. Amelie owned a rather large estate in the hills in southern France.

She had inherited the plot when her parents died. She didn't care to remember any of it, as it would always bring back those horrible dreams. However, spending time with Tryst, would allow her to forget about the horrors she'd faced and instead the feelings would be replaced by a childhood she'd never had. It was refreshing to her to spend time with such an innocent soul. Tryst was the only other person she had loved, as a little sister figure that she never had, Amelie could bond with her and talk about childish things.

As such, today's conversation was about love and family. Her recollections of her family were sub planted by the little girl's memories, which were more refreshing than Lili's. Sometimes she'd wished that she and Tryst could just go somewhere else and be a family of their own. Amelie's retribution would not allow that, would demand justice and so as it was, she'd continue on the course of actions that would place her next to her target, a town mayor that resided in the states. Lately she'd been traveling there a few times every month, carefully picking the stage for her next mark.

She had learned all that she needed when she shacked up with a legionnaire fanatic. He was a rebellious, cocky and more importantly well-trained special ops soldier for the army of France. They would go out to the countryside and practice sniping targets at six hundred meters. She'd convinced him to teach her close quarter combat, military covert tactics and espionage. She was into it. At the time, she was filled with hate and regret. Later when he was serving a tour, she'd gotten word that he'd been KIA. Once she heard that, she raided his weapon cache and took most of his notes. That was just a little over three years to date.

After getting everything ready for her trip, she loaded her BMW with her luggage. The cover story was done and she was expected to arrive in Massachusetts tomorrow. She got into the car and drove towards Paris. She needed to make a stop though and so she left early in the morning instead of waiting until that afternoon.

* * *

Amelie arrived the cemetery where her parents where buried. She walked along the path amidst many cracked and weathered head stones. Names of people long forgotten by their lineage, many of them didn't even have flowers adorning the pots placed at the base of each grave. It made her sick to her stomach that these people took for granted the lives that where given to them by their now lost heritage.

Her own thoughts lingered on the possibility of her own future in regards to family. She sighed and realized that those thoughts would never happen. She could not see past next week let alone think about five years from now. She couldn't imagine anything other than her current existence.

She stopped at some well-polished statues of a man and a woman embracing. She thought that it had been good choice of a head stone and her admiration for the artist who sculpted them grew every time she gazed upon his work. Then, when she had chosen the statue, she had no idea that it would come to be an unwritten epitaph of her parents. For as long as she could remember, her parents' love had always shone wherever they were together. She knew that they were happy where ever they rest. As long as they had each other in the after life, Amelie would find comfort in knowing that. The statues represented their love for each other and she was as happy as anyone could be for the choice in the head stone.

Amelie bent down and lazily touched the earth where her parent's remains where buried. She got on her knees and rested her cheek on the ground. It was cold and the feeling was a welcomed one. It mirrored her heart and she realized then that she didn't want to be this way. She had little choice in the matter—she thought, they made her who she was and her stern decision to hunt these makers down was as nagging as it ever had been.

For a long moment, she sat there on her knees. It was fast approaching fall and this day marked the first day that the leaves on the trees that dotted the cemetery would begin to shed. As the morning morphed in to afternoon, it started to rain leaves. The thin blanket of foliage on the ground was only disturbed by the quickening of the wind. The mood was right and today would be one of those days where she would speak her mind to the ever-silent sentinels of her mom and dad.

"I miss you guys so much," she said allowed.

The sound of her voice breaking the calm serenity of the cemetery seemed inappropriate and she thought that she could hear her mother give her a hush. Like a mother would a crying child. The echoes were carried in the wind and it made her give pause to the savor the sound. It has been too long for her to remember, but the sound of her mother's voice echoed in her head and that brought back vivid memories to Amelie. She closed her eyes and mentally forced herself to hold on to the memories. It was soothing to her and she could hear it like someone was speaking into her ear. She felt a flush of warm breath against her cheek.

"Avenge us, my daughter" it was her mom's voice. Amelie opened her eyes a little startled and straightened up to look around. There was nobody in sight. The wind picked up again and blew the leaves across the grass. It made a rustling sound and Amelie thought she heard the whispers again. She dismissed it as her imagination playing tricks on her. Amelie got up and gave pause one last time to her mother and father resting at her feet.

It was getting close to her flight and she thought that even though she wanted to spend more time here, she needed to get going. She needed to avenge them for the infraction forced against her parents.

* * *

Special Agent Jim Manone was a young man who just turned thirty-four; he was in his prime and took it upon himself to be matriculate. Jim was the type of guy that paid attention to detail, he didn't miss anything and he prided himself of that. Because of his obsession for perfection, he climbed the ranks of the FBI's homicide division extremely fast. One of the best field agents, he was put into middle of the action all the time on every case he worked.

His neatly combed hair was a deep red and his clean-shaven face belied his age. Jim always sported the finest of suits. Even his standard dress attire was of a black sheen. He was the role model for most of the younger agents on the force. Jim loved the notion of being a role model for the other agents. It boosted his already inflated ego. In addition, it helped with the women.

Jim was assigned to unusual homicides in the cases that crossed interstate lines. His primary assignments involved mainly serial killers. Most of the victims of killers had something in common such as gender, or color, sometimes even underlying points of interest like maybe locations or names. The more radical ones usually followed some biblical prophecy or some stupid nonsense like that.

Therefore, when the black dagger case landed on his desk with out a parachute, he was rather confused. His senior field agent in charge insisted that he take this case. There was no background what so ever on any of the five deaths. No information on the killer other than he'd always left a black serrated knife on the scene, usually in the body. All he really got was six pieces of paper in a manila folder labeled *'black dagger assassin'*. He started to cross-reference the five stiffs in the folder but nothing out of the ordinary came up.

Two cops that were partners, one retired commercial helicopter pilot, one disabled man in a nursing home, and the last was a medical surgeon for Chicago's finest. None of them had been related to each other.

Jim sent the evidence down to his forensics lab for testing; maybe he would get lucky and find some *DNA* the previous case workers might have missed. There wasn't much to work with, with so much as a description of the any suspect or suspects; he had little to work with. He was in the process of questioning the victims' background when his phone rang. Jim paused a moment to pick it up, he had a feeling that it was more bad news. He let it ring a few more times and then reluctantly picked it up.

"This is Agent Manone, can I help you?" he answered.

"Yes, this is forensics... I think we have something." The female voice replied.

"I'll be right down" Jim concluded.

Man she was a hot one. Jim always loved listening to her voice on the phone. Sometimes he would even have forensics re run tests when she was on shift. The FBI always had hired good-looking people and he'd never complained. One of these days he thought, one of these days she is going to give it up. He smiled at that thought.

When Manone entered the lab, he was greeted by a rather attractive red head. Her hair was tied on a bun atop her head. Under her while lab coat, she wore slim causal slacks. Jim could see her pelvic bones on her hips being softly accentuated by the pants she wore. Her blouse was neatly ironed and it spoke of someone that was matriculate and disciplined. It was topped off with a low cut 'V' neck that was adorned with three buttons. The top one was undone.

He licked his lips.

Despite her thin-wired reading glasses, Vanessa still looked stunning with even toned skin that brought out her deep hued hair. She had faint freckles dotting her cheeks, and he thought they were just the cutest little things.

"Jim!" he'd heard her declare.

"Oh… sorry, I was distracted." Jim managed to spurt out.

"Yeah, I bet…" She trailed off.

Vanessa walked over to a dish that contained some metal fragments. The lab was neatly cleaned and there were different types of machines with magnifiers and telescopic devices. X-Ray scans occupied the walls and in her area and he saw some of the names. They were his victims' names.

"So… what did you find?" he prompted.

Vanessa shifted through some paperwork and pulled one out. "This is the lab report on these fragments here." She paused. "The surgeon removed these from one of your victims."

"Fragments…? Like pieces of metal, fragments?" Jim questioned.

"Yeah… The compounds in these fragments are made of your typical steel, but there are traces of explosive material." She went on "Like from a grenade…"

"But none of these people were in the military, I checked that." The denial was clearly written on his face.

"I'm telling you this man has seen combat." Vanessa stated rather bluntly. "And you need to check again."

"Sometimes someone's body can say more about them in death than records can say about their lives." She hinted.

"Look, this victim over here, was shot three times..." She was getting really excited now.

"These men had been in the military. And I bet if you talk to someone in DC, they might come up with some purged records, classified documents, or something."

Jim took this all in and started to think about the possibility that these men were part of some shadow unit. He'd heard about them before, through stories back in basic training. However, the military never confirmed that they even existed. Though it would seem, he'd have to uncover a secret his government wanted to keep hidden.

The problem was that, the members of these shadow units never existed. Nothing from their recruitment to their retirement was ever documented. Either he'd have to find someone that would confess, or he'd have to take the case to the trashcan.

"I'd have to say that some pretty fine work there professor," he said with lightly laced bravado. "How about I reward you, maybe take you out to dinner tonight?"

"Ah... I think not Agent Manone." She suggested. "Besides, I don't think you can handle someone like me.

"Oh really... And what exactly is the definition of someone like you, Doctor?" He prodded.

She gave him a sour look in reference to the blatant mislabel he used.

"I think we are about done here, is there anything else I can do for you, like maybe fetch your slippers or something?"

"Seriously, thanks for your help Ness." He said sincerely. "I don't know what kind of agent I would be without my brilliant technicians."

"Like they always say, behind every great man there is an even greater woman." She countered with a smirk.

Jim was pushing her buttons and wanted to see how far she would allow him to take her. It was usual for him to be this way, and he knew that she was used to him doing that. However, that wasn't the point—he thought, it was more of wearing her down and he believed that eventually she would cave in. He just smiled as he left the laboratory.

Chapter 4: Close Call

"This is the captain speaking… we are about to land at J.F.K airport. The local time is seven O' five pm. Our current weather is fifty-five degrees, a little chilly for the early autumn visitors. I hope you have enjoyed your flight, and please fasten your seatbelts. Thank you for Flying Air France." The Flight sounds system chirped.

Another visit to the states she mused. As the plane descended onto the runway, Amelie thought about the pain, her experiences, and the traumatic events that shaped her future. This is how she prepared for her next task. Gathering up her rage and hatred and focusing it onto the attention of her plans.

The plane landed with a whooshing thump. She heard the skid marks as the tires hit the concrete. The plane's engines whined up as the directional covers closed on the turbine vents. The plane started to shake violently and she felt that she was going to throw up. There was a bag there and even though it had not, she knew that it all could change if the ride got bumpier.

The plane slowly taxied along the runway and Amelie peered out the window to see all the people working on the tarmac. After the plane circled around, it was pulled into the boarding gate. The tracker used was like the ones at *Charles de Gaulle* airport. The flight attendants started to open the cabin and excused rows at a time so that the passengers could get off. Soon it would be her turn and she could almost anticipate her relief. Almost there—she thought.

Thank god for that... She was out of the plane and walking through the terminal when a man grabbed her by the arm. She was startled and moved away out of his grasp.

"Excuse me... but you dropped this." The man interrupted. He was holding out a piece of paper.

Her eyes locked onto the paper and she tried to figure out if it was her notes or something else. She went numb inside. She gingerly reached for the paper, expecting the man to try to arrest her. It didn't happen. The man nodded and made eye contact for a brief moment. She returned the gaze quizzically.

This man was rather handsome. He smelled very pleasant and he was well groomed despite his chiseled features. His hair was long by men's standards and it radiated a deep brown hue. He wore a relatively bland button up shirt with western style pockets. His pleated slacks were clean and pressed. His demeanor spoke of a well-disciplined and focused person. He seemed rather confident in himself and when he spoke, the words were smooth.

"Coming here on business?" he questioned.

Amelie didn't know how to respond. After all, he could have looked at the paper. It was in French so she wasn't worried too much. What would she do if he spoke French? Her paranoia was getting the best of her, and she forced her panic down.

"Désolé, excusez-moi !" she replied, hoping that the French would throw him off. He stood there just smiling. Good maybe he'll leave me alone now—she thought.

"Parlez-vous Français?" he timed perfectly. A look of shock stretches across her face. However, it was quickly replaced by a composing smile.

"Pardon, Monsieur..." she ended.

Amelie walked off then, glancing at the paper… it wasn't in French but English. Her command of the English language was good, some would even think that she was from Louisiana by her accent, but her reading of some of the more complicated words was a bit troublesome. The paper read *'I can't help but not notice you. Would you care for dinner?'* There was a number on it too.

Was this man genuinely interested in her? She couldn't help but wonder. She thought about calling the number and scheduling a date but realized that it would be a mistake. She didn't want to get anyone involved in her little hunt. More importantly, she didn't know if she could trust him. She dismissed the notion rationalizing that he didn't have anything to offer in the first place.

She turned around and continued walking to the taxi pick up. She needed to make a phone call first though. Just then, something caught her attention. I was a man dressed in a gray trench coat. She had seen him get on the plane in Paris and noticed him getting off the plane at the terminal. Amelie had seen him when she was talking to the other guy, and now she was noticing him going to the same place as her. Her paranoia was climbing now and she thought that he might be the one that had always shadowed her movements.

Amelie pretended not to notice the man, in fact she purposefully moved in a way that normal people would not. She went from the baggage to the terminal, then back to baggage. Every so often, she would look behind her, checking to see if he was still following her. By the time she reached the baggage the second time, she lost him.

Maybe it was just paranoia and not her instincts. Maybe he had caught on to her tactics and backed off. To any event, this was the first time she had seen someone that she suspected was there, following her, marking her movements and taking extensive precautions not to be seen.

Later that day, she'd taken a taxi to the bus station where she waited for her route to Boston. Watching the scenery go by through the bus window, she could not help but think about France, how she loved the country there. It was a stark contrast to where she was now, but alluring at the same time. She thought about Trystine and her innocence. Somehow, Amelie managed to separate her longings from her realities. When she was away on 'business' she turned into a killer, she was calculated, refined and patient.

When she was at home with Trystine, she was giddy, happy, and anxious. It was as if she had become two different people. All she could hope for was that the previous would die with the last one. Then she could move on and pursue her dreams. Dreams… what dreams? She had been so consumed with her vendettas that she never thought about her future. Before she knew it, the quiet darkness took her.

* * *

After looking over the preliminary reports, Jim realized that every single victim in the file was military, but from what branch and why was there nothing on these guys' records? It was all confusing to him. He had to figure this out. He turned to his computer and clicked an icon. GroupWise mail opened and he began to fill in the address. As he typed out his message, he also mumbled what he was typing. It was a sort of habit that allowed him to keep his train of thought while using email.

"My friend, informer… I seek information on five people that have come up dead in my case. Could you please find the reason why these people's military careers have been erased?" He paused for a moment. "And if you are interested, I'll be in DC this weekend, you can reach me at my office number there. Attached is the list of the five men I need information on."

"Pee Ess, can you include any information on what platoon or squad they belonged to as well as getting the rest of the names in the unit in question?" He stopped to tap his chin. "Thanks, I owe you one."

Jim got up and grabbed his suitcase, car keys and a few other things; he had a road trip to go on and wanted to get a head start. It was a long drive from Langley to Washington.

* * *

She heard the screams again, and the guns… the men were hitting her mother. She heard herself say *papa?* Then the man closest to her said something. *Shut up bitch!* Then he moved over to her wielding a rifle. He didn't point it at her, but instead hit her with it. She heard her dad, heard gunshots. The whimpering of her mother echoed through the darkness. It was a wave washing ashore and breaking on the coast of her soul. She tried to get up but she couldn't.

She was being pushed, shoved and suddenly she was awake. The man that stood above her, towering, was trying to wake her. The bus had stopped and when she got up, she realized that they were already in Boston, at the bus terminal. The bus driver explained to her that she had slept the whole trip.

He'd pulled into the terminal station, unloaded everyone, and had time to take a fifteen-minute break for a smoke, thinking she would wake and get her belonging. She was there, still snoring away, in a deep trance of her nightmares.

Quickly composing herself, Amelie grabbed her suitcase and walked out of the terminal. She was accustomed to walking and it was not a nuisance to walk a few blocks to find a motel. She checked in and for the next few days, studied the motel and everyone that came and went. She was getting the feel of the area, and started to figure out her best course of escape incase she needed to run. She did that everywhere she went. There were a few close calls, because of her disciplined habits and keen sense of intuition, Amelie was able to disappear when those times arose.

Spending countless hours monitoring the address where her package was delivered, Amelie was convinced that nobody suspected anything unusual. She picked up the rifle and went to a remote area of the country to inspect the weapon. Time for a little target practice—she thought.

Assembly of the rifle was easy, she managed to beat her all time record of having that thing ready in less than seven seconds. Not that speed meant anything… if she were in a situation where it would warrant speed, she'd just use a pistol instead. After all, she didn't have anything to loose… or did she?

The question smacked her in the face. Lately, she'd been subsiding in her vindications. She found that she was becoming more and more normal in her constant battle of hatred and remorse. Remorse was winning and she felt good about that. With each kill, Amelie was in fact killing off demons that plagued her. As of late, the dreams have been less consistent and with each dream, she'd remembered more.

It was all coming together for her. She would start here, move to her two other marks and then go back to France. Still though, she still could not determine if she had been tracked through out this ordeal. Always looking over her shoulder and wondering if she had been made. The sensation was the tickle at the back of her throat that kept her alert and she had grown accustomed to it. Lately though, that tickle had become more of a chap.

She had a few weeks to stage his retirement plans. He was up for re-election and his campaign was starting soon, she planned to take him on one of these occasions. As she sat there and thought about the encounter, she played out in her mind. She thought about all of the aspects of the event. How they would occur and where she would be when they occurred.

She felt the cool temperature of the rifle's muzzle as it rested on her cheek. She had not fired it yet. It smelled clean, well oiled, just as she had left it when it was placed in the box. She admired its perfection, it was meant to do one thing, and it did it well. She was almost jealous though… If this PSG-1 had a soul, it would never question its existence. The rifle would know exactly what to do, and how to do it.

There were no gray areas; it was all black and white to Mr. PSG-1. Glancing at the rifle, she knew that it would perform as a surgeon would. Slightly modified to fit a ten-centimeter suppressor, the barrel was shortened enough to compensate for the extra weight. Amelie shouldered the weapon and looked through the scope. She steadied herself and controlled her breathing, then eyed the apple atop the rock she'd placed it upon and steadied herself. Just under four hundred meters, the apple was completely oblivious to its eminent death. A few adjustments and the image would be in focus.

She could feel the tension in the trigger, could hear it speaking to her. It beckoned her to release it. To allow it to do what it was meant to do. Steady now—she thought. The rifle pleaded at this point, it wanted to fulfill its destiny, and she knew that with her intervention, it would succeed.

She smiled at that.

Even the thought of this thing having a soul made her giggle just a little. It was rather silly even, but the contrast to what it was made the thought intriguing. She squeezed the trigger and felt the rifle slightly kick. Smoke came from the barrel she peered through the scope to see a now destroyed apple on a rock.

Wait! She didn't even register the sound… the whisper if its release under shadowed the recoil and its reloaded chamber. Her smile went wide. She picked up the spent cartridge and dismantled the rifle. I have to give you a bath later.

* * *

Jim arrived in DC five hours earlier than expected, of course, this was hastened by the fact that his contact in DC actually found exactly what he'd been searching for. It was early in the AM and he went straight to the FBI offices in Washington, to the office of Lisa Hunsaker. She was an old flame in his life that caught on to his promiscuous activities. She didn't care too much at the time, just was expecting more from a man with his charisma. He thought that she would stop seeing him, but she insisted that they remain exclusive with no commitments. He liked that, but it all ended when he was reassigned to Langley to head up the new division of unsolved homicide cases. How he missed her passion and every time he came to DC, he hoped to rekindle that spark, but she'd grown away from him and never seemed interested. Like a cat bored with an old play toy.

He brought all his files with him to compare notes with what she had found on this 'shadow unit'. He stood in front of her office, straightened his tie, checked his breath and sniffed his coat to see if he smelled. All was good. He knocked on the door.

"Come in, it's open..." the muffled door responded. Jim opened the door. Before him stood a well-endowed tall blonde and she was steaming hot! She was sitting at her desk going over some files when he entered. Jim immediately noticed the shape of her breasts underneath her off-white shirt and he imagined how they would struggle to get out. She didn't even look up, but instead adjusted her glasses and casually brushed her dangling hair over one of her earlobes. She wore black, always wore black and it looked good on her.

"Well, hello to you too" he spouted sarcastically. She didn't even respond but rather continued to comb over the files in her face.

"Have a seat; you might want to hear this." The seriousness in her tone commanded him to obey.

"What is it?" he implored.

"Your shadow unit" she replied. "They were in fact CIA. You were looking in the wrong agency."

Jim looked puzzled. He couldn't have over looked something as obvious as that. Maybe he was getting rusty. Just as he thought that, she continued.

"Did you even check the CIA database?" she scolded. "Maybe you are getting rusty." He scowled at her.

"Well, I hope that is what you are looking for." She added.

"It is… now I have to put all this together…" he mindlessly chattered while looking through the paperwork. "Thanks hun, I owe you dinner tonight." He said abruptly and exited the room.

"Not if I can help it!" She shouted to him.

Jim wasn't listening, he had found out that the entire unit was only twelve agents; they worked covert ops on missions in Europe. All retired now and everything they did was in this file… he didn't have the clearance to read this, but Lisa did. She didn't know that his clearance was reduced last year.

To any event, he had searched the CIA database but, because of his clearance level, nothing turned up. Now though, all that changed. He had what he needed to link these five deaths together. Of the twelve that were in this unit, minus the five, five remained. Two died on other missions in the field and the rest retired or disappeared only to turn up later in his lap. Something big was happening and he could sense it.

Later that day, he checked into a hotel down the street and he focused on reading every little detail about the file. He wanted to burn the information in his head so that when or if something was significant, he would be able to better piece the story together. These people were brutal and he found himself amazed that the CIA let them get away with all that they had done.

This team was responsible for assassinations of political influences across Europe, kidnapping of inventors of leading technology, interception of documents to forge alliances, blackmailing foreign officials and even threatening Parliament at one point. These people were hardcore—he thought.

Who ever was knocking these people off was way out of his league. Russian mafia, Yakuza, or something more—he speculated. Among many of their exploits, Jim read something about them killing a French man for working with the Russians on some secret project, of course this was before the fall of the *USSR*.

It was brutal and he felt sorry for the little girl that was left behind. These men deserved to die, but it wasn't his place or the killers to pass judgment on them. The law was the law. One of the names caught his eye, and he realized that this man was important. He'd heard the name before back in September of 2001. He made a quick phone call to the offices of the FBI, Boston and inquired about the politician. He was alive and well by their estimates.

Jim looked through all of his notes on the black dagger file and nothing seemed to create any patterns. Something triggered him to look at the original enlistment list from the 80s. The men were listed by rank in the military not first or last name, as the usual methods. He compared these to the order the men were found dead. He had a pattern. That would prove the assassin's next target would be... Jim's eyes went wide. He grabbed the phone again and called the Boston office.

Chapter 5: Its time

Amelie arrived in Danvers where she would be living for the next few weeks. She planned to use her cover to live with an old woman that was registered in the foreign exchange program. After getting set up with Matilda, she would begin the first stages of her plan.

The home was not hard to find and Amelie was satisfied that this woman lived on a large plot of land. It almost seemed perfect for what she needed.

She walked up to the door and gave it a sturdy knock. A few moments later, a short old woman answered the door.

"Hi, I am Stephanie..." Amelie paused. "The exchange student assigned to stay with you?"

"Ah... yes, come in, come in sweet dear." The old woman responded with delight.

She was older than Amelie had thought; her face gave way to the passing of time. Her stark white hair was short and seemed to be neatly curled. She wore a white and green mid dress with flowers all over it. She scooted along with a walking aid and every time the walker would clank on the hardwood floor that made her want to cringe.

She seemed kind and gentle. Amelie was curious about the old woman, where was her husband? Does she have children? Amelie found herself pondering about what kind of life this old woman might had lived.

The house was well kept, with old paintings that littered the walls. They depicted farmhouses and barns from the early eras of history. The warm glow from the sun seemed to invade every corner of the house. The light reflected off the brass lamps and the old marble fireplace that decorated the living room wall. There was a sense of pride in the home and Amelie could feel the love that lingered within its walls.

The mantle had pictures of people and Amelie lazily gazed over each one. She looked through the windows of time that the photos captured. The faces were foreign to her but she could see the joy that was behind the souls they depicted.

Amelie almost smiled as she approved of the life that she seen before her, almost. She started to think about her own life. In comparison, it was different from the one she now viewed. She fought hard to stop the sorrow she was feeling at that moment and concentrated on other things.

"I'd hate to be so bold for asking but its kind of important..." Amelie broke the silence in the room. "I need to register for school tomorrow, could you drive me to Boston?"

"Honey, I haven't driven in years..." Matilda said. "Hell, my car rarely gets used but on the weekends."

Matilda looked at Amelie for a brief moment.

"I have an idea, why don't you just take it for as long as you need" Matilda said at length.

Perfect!

"The keys are by the door there. Get yourself settled in first and then you can be on your way." The old woman said over her shoulder.

"Merci beaucoup!" Amelie said after her.

"Before you go, I need to give you a list of groceries you'll need to pick up this week's dinners, if that's ok with you?" Matilda said.

"Thank you again Mrs. Scott." Amelie said cheerfully.

It was time to do some research.

* * *

She watched as he performed his speeches... noted all of the few bodyguards that loosely surrounded his campaign. He was running for the Senate and not considered a far left by American standards so his assassination was not expected. Still though, the secret service added some small presence on his campaign trail.

Her ex had taught her how to find secret service, he used to make fun of them on the tele when they watched the pathetic presidency elections. She didn't forget. This would prove to be one of the most difficult tasks in her overall mission. The timing had to be right and she thought about attempting it tomorrow, it would be the last time for another week and she didn't want to stay here another week.

It was too dangerous; she was always told that if you stay in one spot too long, you would eventually be discovered by the most idiotic of things. She applied that theory to what she was doing, but he was talking about field combat. Well to her this was field combat, of a more urban type—she mused.

Testing the reflexes of these men, she clicked a button on a remote control and pop! The hotdog stand in the crowd just blew its motor. The men jumped onto the mayor extremely fast, two other agents drew their weapons and scanned the crowd. A car moved in from the street and pulled up along side of the campaign platform, they ushered him into the car and they sped off. The two remaining secret service men moved about the area looking for anyone with a gun. From a distance she could see them looking at the hotdog stand and surmising that it was not what they expected. They relaxed.

She was confident that once they found out the source of the explosion, they would call it a false alarm and not think anything of it next week. She laughed at how predictable these Americans were. Oh well, I'd better be going—she thought. She had to plan the next few encounters if she were to get back to France and back to Tryst.

It was curious to her, that she was thinking about the little girl more often and found it pleasantly odd that she was becoming attached to Trystine. She cared more about her than anything in her life and when she was with Tryst, she felt normal. That revelation surprised Amelie... she didn't know how to handle it. For as long as she could remember, Amelie was filled with hate. However, it all started to slip away one day at a time. She was getting sloppy again and the more time she spent with Trystine, the more careless she got.

* * *

Determination set her in motion that day and she went instead to find the next mark that was in DC. Her first mark has a man that owned a pawnshop downtown and she had no problems in finding its location on the internet. She planned to pay him a visit in the middle of the week. She would come back for the Senator on the following weekend when their panicked state turned to normal. Patience would seem to be the better ally than haste. After knocking off the pawnshop owner, she would attend another visit to her next objective, Mr. Marcus Johan who also lived in the same town.

* * *

Jim arrived in Boston the following day, it was an emergency so he'd gotten permission to have the FBI transport take him there first thing in the morning. When he arrived at the FBI offices in Boston, he found that they had already alerted the Mayor. The Mayor explained to the FBI that they had an 'incident' yesterday. The police confiscated the hotdog stand until the mess was cleared up.

Jim ordered the forensics team to investigate the stand on a hunch and his hunch was right. They found the remains of some type of receiver in the whole mess of burned engine parts. The Lab rats said that it was Russian made and that enforced Jim's theory that it was in fact the Russian Mafia behind all these killings. But why? What motive did the Russians posses that spurred them to kill ex CIA agents? Of all their various missions, He'd never read anything on the KGB or the Kremlin. It just did not make sense.

This was getting more and more mysterious to him and he rationalized that either there was something bigger at work here or he was wrong. Since the evidence pointed to the Russians he was almost positive that it was the former and not the latter. He needed more information and it was going to be a long week indeed.

* * *

Amelie arrived in DC and didn't even bother to stop for a hotel room and instead; she went straight to the pawnshop. It was late and she expected the shop to be closed, it wasn't. She walked in and the store was void of people. There were all sorts of junk stacked on shelves with price tags on them.

She walked through the shop and pretended to look for something that she needed. She noticed that the man behind the counter was the one she was looking for. Her heart jumped, this man was the one that had hit her with the stock of his rifle. She felt the all too familiar pumping of adrenaline through her veins. She made a once around the store looking for anyone that might deter her effort.

The man behind the counter was a sorry sap, unshaven and wearing dirty smelling rags. He was overweight and she could see the tattoos on his forearms. Yes, he was definitely the one. She walked up to him and she could see through the cage, that he had a gun strapped to his waist.

She was not worried that he would recognize her, thirteen years of maturity was as good a disguise as the wig she wore. Even though it didn't matter, his life was forfeit anyways. She smiled.

"Excuse me; do you have any working computers?" She timidly asked.

The man spoke in a rather gruff voice, he sounded like his throat had collapsed at one point.

"Yea, sure little lady… right over here." He replied. "The names' Cliff"

He came out from behind the counter and moved over to another counter. She was right behind him and she drew out her knife. They approached the entrance of the building and just as she was getting ready to slit his throat, the door opened.

"Ah… Marcus, I was beginning to think you wouldn't visit after all these years." Cliff addressed the new customer.

"Why would I ever not come and see you, of all people!" Marcus replied.

She recognized the face and the name as one of her targets, and she thought, how could my luck get any better? She grinned at her fortunes.

Amelie realized that she was close enough to strike and so she stabbed out. The knife silently punctured his artery, it was completely imbedded in his neck and she released it. Her right arm reached for the gun at the man's side and she let the falling body's weight draw the pistol for her. She could measure the look on Marcus's face when he realized his best friend was dead. She marveled in that look of shock, almost enjoyed it.

The way it struck his face instantly was a satisfying feeling and she found that it felt good to know that he remembered her.

The body fell and up went her arm as she took aim. It seemed like an eternity as she watched the sight move up to his face. She didn't even focus on him but rather the end of the sight, to be sure that it was inline with him. Just one shot, *BANG!* Then two more for good measure, *BANG! BANG!*

His shock was doubled as he realized what had just happened. He was numb all over but that didn't matter, for all he knew he was just standing there. He could not see anything at all, his vision went black and the burning image of her silhouette was all that he remembered before the end.

She dropped the gun and looked at the dying man before her feet. He was grasping onto what little shred of life left in him. Gurgling and gasping for air, he tried to stem the free flowing of his blood by holding the wound. It was no use. His body went limp and the tell tale pumping of his blood stopped signifying that his heart pushed its last reflex.

It was over in a matter of seconds and she was satisfied. Just three left. Amelie locked the door and turned off all the lights to the shop. She removed her gloves and put them in a tin trashcan. Some of his blood got on her left hand as the knife went in. She doused the gloves with some lighter fluid that she picked up from a shelf and lit it with her lighter. She watched it for a good while as it burned. She was sure that the gloves were completely consumed and reduced to ash. She exited the building from the back and walked away from two of her now gone demons.

* * *

Amelie drove down the highway in Matilda's car thinking about tomorrow's events. She had planned on taking these last two guys out later on in the month, but fate played its hand and she adapted. She always adapted to the situation. It worked out in her favor though and she was already devising plans to compensate for the extra time. She had almost four days to plan her next hit. This time she would watch the target's home and note every little detail. She needed to be more careful than before. The Mayor's protection has probably doubled in the past week and Amelie needed all the information she could get.

She dropped the car off at the train hub early in the morning and took a bus to Boston. She wasn't tired so the trip was rather boring and she used the time to go over her plans. Matilda had granted her the use of the old convertible. It wasn't new but the car did its job well.

Amelie spent the rest of the day going over the escape routes she mapped out. In order for this to go smooth, she needed to be aware of every little detail. Such things like response time of the local authorities, secret service and the FBI needed to be known. No doubt, she would encounter them eventually but Amelie was prepared.

Her plans were falling into place with ease and Amelie was satisfied with their outcome. She was growing weary of all this death and getting this business over with and back to her friend was all that mattered at this point.

Oh Trystine, how does your soul cope without having any parents? How do you live your life on the streets so stoically and resiliently? The thoughts were so familiar to Amelie, but Trystine's cheerfulness and innocence were as foreign to her as the city she now stayed. She wanted to be Trystine and wanted to posses that carefree spirit that shone in her every step. The gleam in Trystine's eyes from the morning sun always seemed to soften Amelie's heart.

She had picked out her spot the day before. It was right across the street and Amelie liked the angle. The roof of the house that she would be on had been up for sale and she imagined what it would be like to live there. STOP... she focused her thoughts to the moment. She needed to concentrate on the tasks at hand and lately she's been catching herself daydreaming about what ifs. Her focus was getting blurry and she needed to remind herself about her business. She had placed the rifle on the roof a few days ago and took note of all the traffic in the vicinity. Amelie was sure that she had not been discovered so she continued her surveillance and made out the undercover agents on the street around the clock. The security that these men provided was at its weakest early in the AM hours.

That was all she needed. Amelie would strike then, when the man was getting his morning paper and would be gone before his face hit the pavement. She was on the cusp of his judgment day and everything had to be as planned. Amelie took extra care to cover her motives by driving through the neighborhood, then using a taxi service, and finally walking down the street. Each time, coming to this place and noting the unmarked car.

She'd stay the night in the back yard of the house that was for sale. She closely monitored the occupants of the house. She noted what they did and where they would go. She had been looking for patterns in his habits of her target and was trying to find the prime shot. Always making note of where the secret service parked and at what times the shift changes occurred. It was necessary for the plan to work, precision and calculation were her business and she smiled every time things went according to plan.

Amelie could not underestimate these agents and she needed to be ruthless and thorough if she were to escape when it all went down. This would be the hardest hit of them all—she thought.

She spent the next several hours watching the movements of the Agents, their habits and even the times they went on break. The time would soon come for her to strike and when she did, she needed to be on her toes if she planned to see Trystine again.

* * *

It was morning and Mayor Augustine climbed out of bed. He hadn't seen anything unusual within the past week. Just a little paranoid I guess—he'd thought.

Today was going to be a big day for him and this would mark a milestone to his political career. He got enough backing from the donations to run for the U.S. Senate.

Even though the FBI was watching him, he couldn't help but feel the heightened tension in the air. All the FBI said was that they suspected that he was in terrible danger. Alfred had made quite a few enemies in the past but none of them dared to take action against him. He was not worried about anything and even if the warnings were legitimate, he would never allow someone to intimidate him or retard his progress in becoming president one day.

His wife slept soundlessly beside him the entire night and she moved ever so slightly as he got out of bed, all the while mumbling something. He paid her no heed, as he knew it was just her talking in her sleep again. Walking half tired to the bathroom for his morning shower, Augustine didn't even notice that his hallway window was slightly cracked open allowing the fresh air to filter into the hall.

* * *

Amelie watched as the man rose from his nightly slumber. She didn't even have to worry about the man's wife, during the night Amelie applied a heavy sedative to the woman's nightgown, odorless and extremely effective, the woman would not wake for hours to come.

She felt a tinge of sympathy for his wife, having to wake up to find out that, her husband had been killed. Amelie thought about taking her life too, just to spare her the misery, but then again she had no reason to. She had scoped out the house a few nights earlier and watched as the heavy secret service kept close tabs on her target. She found it curious that the protection doubled in the past few days... She figured that they were just warming up for his big speech.

She had been there all night waiting for him to separate from his wife long enough to die. The sun was not up yet and she was debating whether to just go in there and kill him or wait for him to get up at the same time everyday.

The car on the street had no movement and she wasn't too concerned about them. As usual the backup or secondary patrol, as her ex would call them, was late and that bought her some breathing room.

From her vantage point, she could pluck off anyone in the house if the occupants were in front of a window. There weren't many obstructions around those windows and she congratulated herself for picking the right time. The lawn maintenance crew had just finished pruning the trees yesterday giving way to line of sight with her PSG-1. She was eager to be done with this.

* * *

Jim and his temporary partner, Lane, were on duty today. Their shift had started around midnight and would continue through until around nine am. He'd been too quick to jump on the possibility that this Mayor would be the next target for the Russians.

It was a long and uneventful week and he'd had nothing better to do than to wait for someone to make a move. It didn't come though and he was beginning to think that there was no connection between these killings at all.

It was late, or early depending on how he looked at it. Another hour before the first hint of daytime would peek the skies. He would not approach the Mayor's house until the Mayor and his wife were decent. He waited for the call that he needed to re-secure the house. All in a days work he thought.

Jim was getting a little concerned, for the fourth night in a row, his back up was late over an hour. This division is sloppy, he thought and if it were up to him, he'd have some of these old timers replaced.

"Hey, where is the second unit?" Jim said aloud.

"Beats the hell outa me, they are always fuck'n off." Lane replied. "try'n get'em on the radio…"

Jim keyed up the handset and took a moment to gather his thoughts.

"Charlie two one to Charlie zero six, radio check…" Jim said to the device.

* * *

She focused the scope and adjusted the rifle to follow him as he wandered around the house. She could almost see clear as day with the night vision scope she had mounted in her PSG-1 and was glad for it too, she didn't want to miss the first time. Everything was a bright green in contrast to her almost completely dark surroundings. She waited patiently, ready to strike.

* * *

The Mayor was fixing himself a cup of coffee and he went to the door to get the morning paper. He wasn't feeling well and needed to get some heartburn medicine because of last night's Chinese food.

He opened the door and his heartburn kicked in. He was thinking about going back to the medicine cabinet, but he was already out the door. He might as well get the paper first. Something was wrong though; he felt weak and didn't know exactly why. Was he having a Heart attack? His answer came with another sting to the chest causing more pain. He clutched it and looked to see blood soaking his shirt. He staggered and fell to his knees. Before the Mayor knew what really happened, he'd fell to the ground to never again rise.

* * *

Jim watched as the Mayor opened the door and walked out. He knew what the man was doing and he'd done it every morning for the past week. What caught him off guard was the fact that the Mayor fell to his knees before even reaching the sidewalk.

"SHIT!" Jim grunted and he opened the door to his Crown Victoria. His partner moved also and they both drew their guns. He grabbed his radio and keyed it up for transmission.

"Charlie two one, to control… I need a medic to the corner of Spruce and Wayward Street as soon as possible." He stated dramatically.

When he reached the Mayor, he could see blood coming from underneath him and immediately conveyed this to his partner with some hand gestures. They took cover close enough to the man to check on his vitals. He was dead and the killer was around there somewhere.

He surveyed the situation and calculated the angles of the shooter. He peeked around the tree he was behind and looked for the shooter.

* * *

She watched has he discovered that the man had in fact been killed. She watched as he checked his vitals, waited for the signal that she wanted him to convey to his partner. Yes, he was dead and the secret service agent just confirmed it. He was looking in her direction then and she noticed that he had spotted her. So she gave off a warning shot. She meant to miss him and that was all the distraction she needed to make her escape.

Amelie rolled off the roof of the house she was on and landed quietly on her feet. A maneuver well practiced on her estate back home. Her rifle was strapped on her back and she drew a USP45-SD. She needed to be cunning here, knew that these men were more trained then she.

She had an advantage, they didn't know what to look for, and she had never been seen up until now, at least not yet anyways. She moved along the side of the house and onto the street. She was spotted, she heard the men yelling at her, telling her to stop or they would shoot. It didn't matter. They were far enough away not to get a good look at her.

Just then, another car pulled up in the scene. It veered toward her and stopped. Two more men got out and she let off a few rounds and rolled behind a parked car to her left. She heard their gunshots hit the car. She thought about trying to run for cover along the street, but caught a glimpse of the men moving to the other side. She was trapped. Her decision to return fire was out of survival more or less and she beaded one of the men approaching her from the house. Crouching in a stable position, she took aim and fired three rounds. All of which hit her target. The man fell grasping his chest. He was motionless.

* * *

Jim watched as the form moved from out of the house and ran down the street.

"FBI… STOP… OR I'LL SHOOT" he declared, but the form kept running. He was too far away to trust his aim to be true. His partner, a man named Lane, gave chase without regard for his own safety. Jim radioed in that the suspect was on foot and he needed back up. The other unmarked had been late and Jim was thankful for that, he watched as the car identified the suspect and moved to cut him off.

They exited the vehicle and opened fire on the perpetrator. The assailant rolled behind a car for cover. Jim moved in, everything seemed to act in slow motion and he watched helplessly as the suspect shot Lane. He went down and Jim moved behind his car for cover. He could see

Lane clutching his chest where he had been hit. He looked over the hood of his car to see if he had a chance at the suspect, but he was gone. He heard two more shots and he tried to peak over the hood. He couldn't see anything.

Jim scanned the street and the yards that flanked the suspect's previous position. No good, he cautiously stood up, half expecting to be shot at but it didn't come. He moved over to his partner and checked his wounds. Lane was a seasoned veteran of the FBI and he wasn't even concerned that the vest he wore stopped the bullets. He wanted to neutralize his threat hoping that his attacker would move on to another target until he could get out of the line of fire.

* * *

Amelie was desperate, now she had nowhere to run. One down but there was three more. Another agent approached her side of the car, the third one flanked her position and she was running out of options. She peered under the car to see the man's feet slowly walk around to her location. Crouching low, she took aim at his leg and popped one off. He fell into her view and she finished him off with a round to the head. She moved toward the slain agent then around behind the car and out of view of the other two agents.

The second car was still running and she could hear the chatter of the FBI radio inside. She waited a few moments and watched for the last man's where-abouts. He had moved to the first dead agent. She watched as he pulled the man to his car.

"Merde" she murmured.

She holstered her USP and un-slung her rifle and took aim on the man pulling the still form of the other agent. She fired and the man fell. He didn't move either. The last agent was still on the other side of the car and she knew he had seen her take down the other two. He had nothing else to do but to either wait for her to leave or try to take her out himself. He chose the latter.

With almost blind ferocity, the agent quickly rose to his feet and pointed his firearm in her direction, his eyes searching for a target, there was none. He didn't see her. What he didn't know was that she had moved to the other side of the car he was hiding behind and was circling around behind him. He moved in reverse towards her and she jumped up and let loose one round... he didn't hear it, didn't even feel it as the bullet punctured his skull. All he knew was that she was there, he tried to turn but his body would not respond. His vision of her became red and he felt a warm sensation on his face then he fell into darkness.

Amelie was confident that none of them were still kicking. In fact, she had waited a long moment as usual to see of any of then wanted more. She doubted it though two of the four had fatal injuries and she justified it as them collateral damage. She still had well enough time to execute her getaway, being within in the response limit of the police; Amelie jumped into the squad car and took off. Like the hunter, she rationalized the situation that it would be either her or them, and she intended on living past this day.

* * *

Jim was wounded and he felt the sting of the bullet wound in his shoulder. It hit high enough to miss the vest he wore, yet low enough to go right through his shoulder. It wasn't fatal but he was afraid that if he moved, the suspect would finish him off. This guy was a professional he thought and after he heard the suspect drive off in one of the FBI cars he surveyed the scene.

Lane was getting up and checking his vest. Jim could see that the other two agents were dead; the holes in the back of their heads left him with little doubt. He heard Lane radio in for more medical support and he tried to explain to the dispatch officer what the suspect looked like. Lane didn't get a good enough look at the suspect to get a positive ID. They even called in air support, to try to track the stolen car, but that ended when they found the car in a ditch, burning in a fiery blaze. This assassin was good.

* * *

After crashing the car, Amelie ran across an open field that flanked the neighborhood she had just exited. She could hear sirens and helicopters in the distance. She surveyed the scene and watched as squad car after unmarked car raced passed. She would wait for the all clear and move across from street to street, until she got outside of the targeted perimeter she knew they would set in their search for her.

She took the time to dismantle her rifle and bundle it into a bag. This would allow her to become more mobile incase they found her. Really seven seconds is not along time when you find the right cover, she convinced herself.

With just a few close calls, Amelie was able to penetrate the search zone she knew they'd staked out. She continued to the escape point she planned ahead of time. All was going better than she anticipated.

Just under a mile away was a train yard. There she waited for the predictable quick stop of a cargo train. Unsuspecting engine conductors didn't even see her board one of the cars. The sun started to peek from the skyline and she knew that they would leave for New York soon. She removed the rifle and slid the boxcar door closed. The next stop was a small town where the train would go to pick up some added cargo and then it would continue on to New York. She planned to exploit this moment and grab her car that she had placed there a number of days ago. Thinking ahead was a good thing.

When she got to her stop, Amelie went to her car and stripped all of her clothes and put them in the trunk, she didn't even bother covering up. She opened the front door and grabbed her dress. Wiggling and slipping it over herself, she jumped in the car and drove off. From there she would take the road west to where she was staying. On the way out, she went to the food mart and picked up a few things; bread, milk, eggs, some flour, and even some vegetables. It was cooking time.

* * *

It was still early when the police car pulled up behind her. She was driving the speed limit and using all the proper turn signals when making her turns. The cop was running her plates she knew and felt confident that the car would come back clean. She thought for a minute that she would be discovered, but played cool. He continued to follow her and she knew that he was trying to make her nervous. She played it as usual. The lights flashed and she slowly moved to the side of the road. The cop pulled up behind her and she rolled down the window, grabbed the paperwork and pulled the hammer back on her pistol. The cop came up to the side of the window and she looked at him expectantly.

"Drivers License, Registration and Insurance please" the cop prompted. Amelie presented her Passport as well as the car's registration and proof of insurance.

"I'll be right back..." the cop stated. "Please turn off your vehicle..."

Amelie complied. He was going to run her passport and come up with nothing. She was ready for something like this and even half expected it. The cop returned and he gave her all of her information back.

"In America, we all have to have driver's license, a passport does not give you the right to operate a car on the road." He stated rather loudly.

"I understand officer," she paused "I just went to get some groceries for my host." She smiled at him.

He looked her over and a smile formed across his face. She was remarkably beautiful and her soft tone was accented by the rising sun. He could smell her perfume. It was a spicy and musky yet sweet smelling at the same time. He'd never smelled that kind of perfume before but he was glad he did.

She moved some hair that was blowing in her face over behind her earlobe and he thought he was going to beg. She licked her lips, not in a way that would suggest she meant for him to see, but in a normal way. He felt himself get hard. She had a natural beauty that he could appreciate and he knew she was aware of it. Still though, he found that she was borderline irresistible, had he not been a cop he would consider taking her. If he could, he would arrest her, just too able to spend more time in her presence. He thought it was crazy that he could be so drawn to a young woman half his age.

He stated with a sheepish grin, "Promise me you'll get your license and I won't give you this citation."

Amelie just smiled right back and replied "Thank you officer, for understanding."

The cop walked back to his car and got in, turned off the emergency lights and drove off. Amelie watched the officer as he passed, all the while wearing that sheepish grin.

Chapter 6: Remorse

The next day Amelie sat in her motel room staring at the wall. The cigarette she was smoking was down to the butt and hadn't been ashed since maybe the first drag. The weight of her actions pounded her morality, she was changing, her hatred was leaving her and she felt bad for killing those men.

Weeks ago, she would not care about collateral damage, but today she found that she did care about it. Her eyes were swollen from tears and her cheeks were irritated from her rubbing them all night long. She didn't get any sleep and she was exhausted from yesterday's ordeal. She was listening to the handheld FBI radio she took from the unmarked car. Serving as a warning system, it was all she needed to monitor their communications. Her rifle was dismantled on the floor by the bed and the room smelled of a mixture of gun oil and cigarette smoke.

A few chirps from the radio grabbed her attention. She could hear that two of the four agents were alive and in stable condition. She was slightly relieved at that and at the same time, she started to cry again. Not trying to hold back any remorse, she let it all out. Her body shook as she pouted and all she could do to calm her self was to think about Trystine.

She was like an anchor for Amelie and every time she thought of the twelve year old, she couldn't help but long to see her again. They had a bond of some sorts. Sisters, orphans, and loners they were akin to each other in so many ways, yet their diverse personalities were so opposite that each needed the other for support. Amelie stopped crying then and started to pack all of her stuff for the flight home.

Getting on the plane proved easy enough, she had prepared the lead box for shipping to an address in Naples, Italy. It would be shipped a week from today with specific instructions to pick it up at the location that she had it dropped off. Earlier that year, she had tested out the International mail system by shipping questionable items in similar boxes, none of them had ever been suspected and she was confident that this one wouldn't be either.

Even if they did find out what was in it, it was in no way tied to her. Even the address was made up, so she would not be worried about any discoveries there. Part of being invisible was to never use your real credentials when traveling and she had an impressive array of fake passports and IDs that she used in intervals of months at a time.

She had met someone through her ex that specialized in such things, and with his help, she was able to travel to just about any country in the west without ever being suspected. It had been just a day since her encounter with the FBI, and she caught on the morning news that there was a killer at large but the broadcast said nothing about who the suspect was. She smiled at that, they hadn't found out yet.

As the plane Taxied along the runway at JFK international, she was glancing about, checking for any thing unusual when she caught someone looking at her. She fainted a blush with a smile acting as if she was caught admiring the man she spied. He just turned the other way. It was yet another sign that she was being watched but by who? She wanted to go over to the man and question him, but this wasn't the time or the place. She decided that she would keep an eye on him until she was able to ditch him if he followed her. Just two more...

* * *

Jim and Lane were in debriefing when they heard the news that their attacker had hit two more people in DC earlier in the week. Jim already knew that those two victims were on his list of names. However, what was surprising to him was that he had found out the killer was on video tape. The pawnshop owner always recorded his lobby. It paid off this time for the sake of his misfortunes. The tape was being copied and sent to his location for evaluation. Jim was almost excited to hear the news, finally a break in his case, finally he could measure up this person if he could get some kind of visual match in the Interpol database.

The results were in before he even got out of debriefing. The research tech didn't find a single person in Interpol that reflected the face of the suspect on the tape. Something that intrigued him even more was the fact that the suspect was a she.

He had already fallen victim to her exploits and he never even seen her, It didn't even register to him that she was young, or beautiful. He'd over looked all of that, what he saw before him was some exotic foreign assassin that eluded the finest of field agents. He knew she was dangerous, knew that if he wasn't careful, his bullet wound could be on his forehead. He had no doubts that she meant to miss him the first time, and even the second time. Why did she kill the other two agents? When the hunter corners an animal, the creature becomes extremely violent and will do anything to survive. Jim realized that they were just collateral damage. The agents should have stuck to their training but in the fleeting moments of battle, got careless and forgot everything they had been taught.

This made her even more mysterious to him. He found that he was beginning to admire her. No, it was more respect than admiration. He was wise in thinking that of course, if he underestimated her again he and anyone he was with would wind up dead. That notion did not sit well with him. He had been close to death before, but he took it all for granted. The difference between this assassin and all the others was the fact that he knew how deadly she could be. It was a perilous thought, even to him, a seasoned special agent of the FBI.

* * *

"How could this happen? I want answers!" The director demanded. He was agitated and pacing the conference room floor wasn't calming him down.

"Sir, my assessment of this… person, is that they had everything well planned, extremely intelligent and thorough." Arnie concluded. "I seriously doubt that the field agents knew what they were dealing with then they pulled up on the scene."

Director Sullivan looked at Arnie a long moment, "Well, you'd better find out more about this… person. I want her taken down."

"Yes sir." Was all Arnie could say.

Director Sullivan was a hard man, and as the director of the east coast operations, Sullivan was notorious for screaming and yelling. Arnie's sole job for the FBI was to profile suspects, to get in their head to determine how they think and better understand them. He mulled over all of the testimonies of the police involved, witnesses to killings from Chicago and other locations, and watched the surveillance tape repeatedly to determine what kind of criminal she was.

He knew she was ruthless, remorseless and disciplined. He could see it in her walk. How she scoped out the building before making a move. The fact that the man who was killed addressed her as a new customer led him to believe that she had never been in there before. The way that she handled that unsuspecting visitor in the middle of her attempt told him that she didn't panic, that she was a quick thinker and knew how to take advantage of any situation.

He surmised that this was how she neutralized four FBI agents in less than four minutes, just two minutes shy of their quickest back up response. For some, two minutes can be a lifetime, for others it would be the last moments of freedom. However, for her those two minutes were all she needed to escape. The level of skill she possessed was startling and he would have to focus all of his energies if he were to apprehend her.

There were teams all over the place, with K-9 looking for her through the neighborhoods, Patrol stops of any vehicles driving in the vicinity. They even checked the sewer systems. How did she evade the search effort was a mystery to everyone. All motel and hotels were searched for the suspects weapons and clothing. The sheriff's department as well as the local Boston Police in association with the FBI yielded no arrests, no gun, and no girl.

He was baffled and that's why the director had chewed his ass out. They came to him for answers like that and for the longest time, he'd been studying the case as a favor to his friend Jim who worked at headquarters. Still though, even with the new information on the case... he still could not categorize her methods or train of thought. It appeared as of she were a machine programmed to do one thing. Moreover, there was still the question of motive. His only guess was that she was well trained.

* * *

Gregory and Tom met in a private room in a small town, somewhere down south. They both had heard about the killings if their ex CIA team, and wanted to talk about securing their safety. They could not make any public statements or otherwise alert their stalker. What they planned to do was get all information on the case that the FBI possessed. That's what they were talking about now. They sure as hell weren't going to wait for their assassin to come knocking on the door, no they were going to set the stage themselves. All they needed was the case files and they knew exactly who to talk to get them.

Tom had been looking into some business venture when the news got to him. He immediately called Gregory who was still working as a private detective in Las Vegas.

They both agreed to meet in New Orleans to discuss their options. To Tom's surprise, he found out that Gregory had followed the killings when they started.

Gregory was the only person on the team that took efforts to stay in touch with the others, and when he had gotten news that his friends and acquaintances where dropping of the face of the world, he started to contact the others only to find that some of them had already been killed. He tried to get in touch with Ted but he had already gone home for the day.

Later, Gregory found out that Ted had been assassinated in the middle of the street. The killer took out his home along with his wife. At first, the job looked sloppy but when he had talked to the homicide caseworker, he started to believe that the killer improvised the situation. Finding out that an innocent bystander was murdered for no apparent reason enforced his theory.

They both had agreed on the spot because if location. When they reached the meeting place, Tom and Gregory immediately started plans that would lead them to the small village in southern France where they would use what ever means available to end this threat.

* * *

Jim had the computer geeks clean up a snapshot of the girl in the video, so good they were that the picture almost did her justice. He didn't know that but if anyone seen the now printed photo, they would agree. He ordered that picture to be posted on the evening news. The snapshot was plastered all over the various police departments and other law enforcement agencies all over the US. In a matter of just a few hours, the story was making national headlines.

Jim was satisfied at this and wanted to give her something to think about while she was hiding. He knew she was watching and knew that she would try to run. As soon as the reports came in, Jim would have his specially assembled team to respond. He hoped to capture and not kill the suspect. He wanted so badly to get the assassin that he could see the outcome even before it happened. He had to control her movements, give her no place to hide or run for that matter. She would try, and he would be there waiting.

He didn't know that she had already escaped the country. He didn't know that she was thousands of miles across the world settling in another life that which he had no inkling of. For all Jim knew, she was hiding out in some small town in between here and god knows where.

Jim was going over the new evidence looking for another lead to go on. One thing he started to notice was during the incident at the pawnshop, she was talking to the owner. It wasn't what she said that caught his attention, it was they way she pronounced the words. She was from another country where English was not her first language.

"Mother fucker!" Jim cursed.

"What's that" Lane perked up.

"It would seem that our little assassin friend is from another country..." Jim exclaimed.

"How do you figure that?" Lane was interested now.

"She has an accent." Jim stated. "I need to get an audio professional up here to clean up the sound on this video."

"I'll get someone up here right away." Lane offered.

Just then, the phone rang and Jim picked it up. Lane was on the phone when Jim grabbed a pen and paper. He quickly wrote down a name and a number and handed it to Lane.

"I have someone coming right up." Lane said. "What's this?"

Jim cupped his hand over the phone.

"It's the name and a number of one of the guys on the list; I think he is trying to get access to the case file."

Lane was confused. "What do you want me to do?"

"Call him..." Jim ushered.

"I know that but should I be accommodating or aggressive?" Lane asked.

"Just find out what they know..." Jim prodded.

Lane picked up the phone and dialed the number. It rang for a long while and Lane was beginning to think that nobody was home. A man answered on the other side and Lane immediately started the recording.

"Hello, this is Special Agent Sommers from the FBI, is this Tom?"

* * *

Her plane landed and it was now her turn to exit the plane. The man she was watching had already gotten off, and he gave no indication that he was interested in her throughout the flight. She didn't let that dissuade her however, she knew that he was up to something and if he did not show his face when she left the airport, she would be surprised.

No signs of the man, she grabbed her luggage and went to the long-term check out. It was a few long moments to process the information to get her car out, while she waited while she watched the news, and to her surprise, she seen a picture of herself as being wanted in the deaths of two federal agents and one politician. The photo was a good one but it was not good enough to match her. In the segment, she was also accused of killing two police officers, a shop owner and his customer, and four other civilians.

"Well that changes things a little...," she mumbled to herself.

Amelie started to think about not returning to the US anytime soon. She would have to wait a long while to carry out the rest of her plans. With the trail being as hot as it was, she would have to lay low for a while.

She'd thought about just calling everything off and trying to lead a normal life. Her confusion was nagging at her conscience more and more. It was becoming a bit of a nuisance and Amelie wanted to get this all done and over with.

Someone called her name and at first, she thought that it might have been the authorities, but then she realized that it was the car check attendant. Her papers were processed and she was able to get her car.

She grabbed her keys from the counter and walked to the parking garage. There was no sign of anyone following her this time, but that didn't mean they were not there. She loaded her luggage, jumped in the car and drove from Paris to southern France, the only thing on her mind was seeing Trystine again.

Chapter 7: Recourse

She heard the men talking, heard her father pleading. One man asked for something, a chip… a computer chip. Her dad said remained silent at first but then he said that it had hidden it. She didn't understand.

Then she heard the all too familiar of gunfire, heard the screams and when she came around, she saw that the men had gone. The room was in shambles, her father was laying there, half of his head gone, splattered on the floor. Her mother lay just a few feet away, her clothes were ripped away from her bare form and she could see that her mother was still breathing.

She went to her mom and talked to her, she was crying now and she knew her mom was going to die. Her bones were broken, and she could see bruises along her chest and face. Her arm didn't look as it was supposed to, it was crooked, her side was caved in, and Amelie could see something white poking out of the side of her mom's chest. Blood came from that area and it was fast making a puddle.

She didn't know what to do. "mum?" She whimpered. "Mum... Mum please wake up."

"Run Amelie, get help... I love you, Hurry." Her dying mom whispered. Amelie cried more, and she didn't know what to do.

"My child, you must go get help, please!" her mom continued. Amelie slowly got up, and her mom rested her head on the ground. She ran out the door and into the street, screaming all the while. It was raining and puddles of mud were fast forming in the street. Amelie slipped in one and she landed in muddy water. She struggled to stand and continued running into the street.

"Somebody please help me, my mom is hurt, please!" she kept screaming.

It was in the middle of the night and a heavy down pour of rain was accented by the flash of lightening. It was followed by a thunderous roar and Amelie thought that god was scolding her.

As she ran, she could feel the dreaded gloom wrap around her, smothering her with its entirety, it was no use... nobody came, nobody helped her. Amelie sat in the rain yelling the same thing repeatedly. Soon the rain stopped and the sun started to rise, Amelie still did not find help. She was just seven and her small frame could not support the sorrow it bore through the night, she gave in to weakness and passed out from exhaustion in the middle of the road.

* * *

Amelie was awake now, and she lay there in bed curled up into a ball weeping. She shook violently with the sorrow and grief that was greater than it ever had been. It washed over her, drowning her in its wake. She cried and cried, pleading with god to help her find peace.

In the early hours of the morning, the walls of Amelie's home echoed to her the pain and agony she felt with the sheer stillness of silence. She cried herself to sleep again, this time too deep to dream.

* * *

Trystine knocked on the door but there was no answer, she knew her friend was home but she wasn't answering the door. She knocked again and still there was no answer, so she decided to try to find another way in.

Tryst wanted to spend time with Amelie; she missed her dearly and couldn't wait for her return. Along the side of Amelie's house, Tryst found a small rectangular window from a basement room. It window was cracked open, she was able to open it all the way and she slipped through it with ease. The room looked as if it had not been in for years. Everything was covered with spider webs and dust. There were pictures and rugs on shelves as well as furniture that had been covered by sheets.

The wooden floor creaked as Tryst walked through the room to the stairs. Something caught her eye though and made her pause. It was an old teddy bear, half ripped on one ear, dusty and one of the eyes were dangling off. She gingerly picked up the stuffed animal and inspected it with care. It was brown with a white belly. She shook it a little to get the dust off and continued to the stairs.

The door at the top wasn't even locked and Tryst opened the door slowly. She'd been around the street a lot and she knew how to be quiet when she didn't know what was going on. The house was quiet as can be. It was around noontime and she expected Amelie to be out of bed cleaning, or cooking as she had always done around this time. There was nothing but the faint clicking of a clock was all that revealed life within the room.

She moved along the hall to Amelie's room. She was confident that Amelie would not be angry for her intrusion, so she continued into her room. Amelie was there sleeping on the bed. She could hear the rhythmic sounds of Amelie in her deep slumber. Tryst decided to climb in bed with her and lay down too. Tryst positioned herself so that her back was to Amelie's front. Amelie stirred for a moment then half awoke to pull Tryst into her.

"I've missed you." The small voice quietly revealed and Amelie was happy to hear that.

"And I have missed you too little one." she murmured back, finishing it off with a warm embrace.

The two of them slept that afternoon in each other's company. The peace that Amelie dreamt of was more than she'd ever imagined. It was like a fairy tale to her. No horrible nightmares or re occurring experiences flooded her mind that day. Trystine acted as if she were a shield against Amelie's demons, reflecting the horrors that plagued her soul in the quiet darkness.

* * *

"Everything is set." The man spoke softly. He was talking on the phone with another man that just called him.

"Do you think she knows we are coming?" the voice asked.

"No" he replied. "She doesn't suspect a thing. You should meet me in Marseille tomorrow evening, at the place specified."

Tom hung up the phone, and went back to typing on his computer. The plans were set in motion and soon he would have the intel he needed to terminate this assassin. It was just a matter of time before he found out all the details. Tom finished packing his things and just when he finished, he'd gotten a phone call. It was his source from the CIA and they called to give him what he needed.

Delauney..., Delauney... why does that name sound familiar--he thought aloud. It was strikingly familiar yet at the same time, he could not place the name.

"Anyways, the information will be waiting for you their, All you have to do is pick it up at the hotel desk." The caller instructed.

"Ok, thanks, I owe you buddy." Tom said at last.

"Don't mention it" was all the man said in response.

* * *

Director Motts hung up the phone, He was securing his future and he wanted to make sure that all loose ends where tied nice and neat. Why the team didn't kill the little girl thirteen years ago was not really a question of mercy. It was to prevent exactly what was happening now.

The mission was not sanctioned but ended up being sanctioned because of the link between Charles Delauney and the Russians. He had back forged all the records for the senate' interest with little mentioning of the reason why they were there in the first place. He didn't need this kind of attention in the middle of his career.

* * *

Tom tasked Gregory to do a little surveillance when they arrived in town. The trip the France was a productive one for the two. They read up on the case files Motts supplied as well as information on the local area. It was SOP to them and Tom stopped the think about how much he missed those days.

His team had done many missions in Europe and they knew the languages. They had access to the underground scene and knew whom to talk about obtaining arms. Tom was in charge of that. Nothing special, save for suppressors. They wouldn't need an arsenal of weapons to deal with a lone would be assassin. He was confident that she would not expect them to show up on her doorstep.

Gaining an advantage and using it was one of his primary skills. His field of expertise was to know how to setup a situation to favor him and his team.

This situation was no different for him and Gregory. They would scope out the area, plan a confrontation, and execute it with efficiency and prejudice. She had no idea of what was coming. He hated to have to kill someone for the sole reason of self-preservation, but Motts insisted that they finish this task, something they should have done thirteen years ago.

* * *

That night, Gregory did a little recon at the Delauney home. He noticed that she was not alone as the report said. He tried to determine if there were more than just the two but all he could see was that, along with Amelie, there was a little girl living there too. Was she a sister or a daughter, maybe? No, it had to be a sister. The little one was too old to be her daughter. He studied the two for a long time gauging their awareness and making note of the layout of the house.

He would report this information tomorrow, but for now, he tried to get closer for some audio. He moved along the hillside to the back of the house. They were in the living room so he wasn't too worried about being spotted. There were no neighbors on this hill and Gregory was thankful for that. He wanted to remain invisible for the sake of surprise. If he were spotted now, then their chances of success would be cut in half.

He took extra care to dismantle a tripwire he had almost set off. She was good, he thought. He imagined that most of the house if not all of it were wired for various early warnings. Probably most of the yard was rigged with tripwires like the one he just found. It was surprising to know that she was always on her guard. Maybe she thought that one day, his team would come back to finish the job.

He realized then that what ever went down, it could not be here. She might have guns and the like scattered around the house in defensible positions. That didn't sit well with him and he was determined to survive this.

The night slowly moved on and he was getting tired. He waited though, for them to turn in for the night first. He watched as the lights of the house went out one by one. He watched as the last of the lights that marked the room they were staying finally turned black.

Almost twenty minutes later, he left for the hotel. He and Tom had to rethink their plan and in light of this new information, it would be a cat and mouse game from here on out.

Gregory picked up his cell phone and text messaged Tom. His note was to warn Tom of the situation with her home.

"Situation not good, she is prepared," he wrote.

* * *

Tom felt his phone vibrate and he reached in his coat pocket to check the message. It was from Greg. Tom looked at the message for a long moment. His thought slowly trailed out into space as he thought about changing the plan. He smiled and put the phone down.

Tom started to jot down some instructions for Greg and included some phone numbers. He grabbed the phone again and started his reply.

"Meet me outside at the rear parking lot in 10 minutes."

He pressed send and grabbed his gun.

* * *

Amelie woke up the next morning with plans to take Trystine to the market. She and the little girl were going to celebrate Trystine's birthday with a picnic on the countryside. Tryst was in the living room watching her favorite TF1 episode.

She strolled out of bed and walked to the bathroom, all the while lazily rubbing the weary sleep from her eyes. It was fast approaching noon and she needed to get started on the preparations for Trysts little party.

"Is everything ok hun?" she said aloud.

"Yeah everything is fine mum." Trystine answered.

Satisfied that danger had not come this day, Amelie just continued her morning ritual of a hot shower and a cigarette.

It felt good. The hot running water washed away her weariness and allowed her to concentrate on what was going on inside her mind. It was like meditation and she welcomed the peace it offered. Amelie looked into her mirror that was mounted in the shower. The watery reflection caught her attention and she found herself staring at a new person. It was the same face and the same features, but something was different, changed. Amelie could see a sparkle in the eyes of the woman in front of her. She could see that there was something more to the face that she so long remembered being plagued by the demons within.

She smiled as she realized the truth of it. The demons were gone and she realized then that her future was fast becoming bright. The transformation was seamless and she didn't even realize that it had happened. It puzzled her just a little but Amelie welcomed the notion even more with newfound bliss.

* * *

The day started out good for the two and Amelie would ensure that Trystine would have the best day ever. It was a day she would begin her new life with Trystine. The two would be a family and together they would face the common challenges that families face.

The notion was profound to Amelie. She never thought that she would end up being a mentor to someone so akin yet completely different then her. It was an unexpected encounter for her on that lonely road that dismal day. Just as unexpected as the gradual change that occurred within Amelie.

She caught herself smiling as they drove down the country road to the market just outside Beuvron-en-Auge. There, they would gather the needed things to bake a cake. Amelie was going to invite the orphan's street friends secretly. She had it all planned and there wasn't a thing anyone could do to change that.

Yes, her smile was getting bigger and her rosy cheeks were beginning to brighten with glee.

They reached the market and Amelie dropped Trystine off and went to park her car. The afternoon had crept up on her without warning and she had to rush to get to the market before the place closed for the day. Parking seemed a bit of a chore as most of the spots were taken. Luckily, she found one at the edge of the lot.

* * *

Tom and Greg watched as their target drove into the parking lot. They had been expecting the girl after they got the intel from their hired mercenaries. Shortly after she parted her car, the mercs came into the lot. Tom radioed for them to wait until Amelie got into the market.

"Guys, I want you to meet Greg by the restrooms on the south end of the market." Tom instructed. He keyed the radio so ensure that the transmission was complete.

"Roger that sir, south side, restrooms." The reply came.

Tom signaled for Greg to get going. The started off after the little girl.

Greg moved to the southern part of the market to meet these two mercs. His mission was to usher Amelie towards Tom's location while the mercs would flank her just incase she got any bright ideas. It seemed like a good plan.

However, they didn't entirely know what they were dealing with.

* * *

Amelie was moving through the different stands when she noticed someone following her again. She thought that it was the same feelings that struck her before, when she usually sensed someone watching her after she completed one of her tasks. This time though, it was much different. She actually identified the person watching her. He was an English man for sure, probably from the US. She recognized him as one of her targets and that revelation was a shock. Her keen senses started to turn on and she suddenly was aware of everything around her. She had identified two more men that she didn't recognize. They were respectfully keeping their distance yet still following her.

She scanned the market for any signs of Trystine but did not see the little girl. Amelie thought the worst but quickly dismissed it. They knew nothing of the girl and she was almost sure that Tryst would know what to do when a stranger tried to talk to her, almost.

Her plan was to separate these two men from the first. It wouldn't be too hard considering she knew the area better than they and she started to formulate a plan. Everything started to unfold in her mind as it always did and she searched for areas in the market that were secluded from patrons.

She moved to an area that was off to the side not too crowded and she slipped between two large wooden storage containers.

She peered around the corner looking for the two men that were following her. She watched as they flanked her position. It was perfect, she though. Amelie moved out from her cover in between both men. The one in front of her pulled out a knife and grinned menacingly.

She envisioned the other getting ready to move closer, and the telltale sound of scuffling feet confirmed her intuition. In the blink of an eye, she spun about throwing an inner roundhouse kick behind her and felt her boot connect squarely with the man's jaw. She wasn't looking and as she spun, she moved her head faster and fixing her gaze in the man with the knife, making a full circle, like a dancer would. The man lunged at her neck and she ducked below the man's thrust while punching him square in the solar flexes.

With the same motion, she reached up to knock the knife out of his hands. She heard the knife hit the ground and was satisfied that she had effectively disarmed the assailant. The man bent low and before the man could recover from the blow, she thrust her head upward connecting with the man's face. He went sprawling and before he even fell back she finished the movement with a front kick to the chest, the man fell farther back and was done.

Amelie spun about meeting the first man and he was recovering. She watched as he started to pull out his gun. Spurred into action, she ducked low, grabbed the knife on the ground, and rushed into the man from her crouching position. The blade sunk into his chest and he groaned. His gun went off and people screamed. Amelie wasn't done. She pulling the knife out and reversing her grip, then she reversed her spin and came around to his other side planting the knife deep into his armpit. The gun fell along with the man and she scooped it up. Amelie wiped the blade of the knife clean and placed it in her waist. She released the clip from the firearm and let it fall to the ground. With two quick motions, she was able to remove the slide from its receiver and she dropped both components into the nearest garbage can.

* * *

After disposing of the two unknowns, as her ex would call them, Amelie circled around to look for the third man. The one that she had recognized, she wanted to surprise him for the sake of questioning. After all, this was a new ball game and she needed to know how many players were on this new team. Getting his attention proved easy enough. Getting him to follow her to the ideal location proved to be a bit harder.

It seemed that he was following a predetermined path. Every time she deviated, he would stop and wait. Almost as if he had been spotted by her and pretended to be nonchalant about it, like in those old American comedy movies. It seemed rather absurd but she knew what he was doing.

Her intrigue started to kick in and she wondered how they had found her. She must have made a mistake somewhere down the road. Was it the man at the Airport? She found herself thinking about the different missions she did and where any of them could have gone wrong. It donned on her at that moment. He was distracting her, working her nerves, trying to break her calm a little. She moved the way that she thought he wanted her to go. She was going to play this game with him in hopes that she could improvise and strike.

Amelie spotted Trystine talking with one of her other friends. Amelie quickly move out of her sight, in fear that Trystine would be spotted and maybe later kidnapped for the sole benefit of making Amelie play along with what ever game he had in store for her. The man followed without question. Amelie took him around the village and into some alleys where she could confront him.

She disappeared around a corner and managed to lose him. He searched the nooks and crannies only to find a few rats and mice. She watched from a cracked door as the man spoke into his jacket. How many of them are there, she wondered.

Just as the man was getting ready to exit the ally, Amelie emerged. He stopped and turned around when he heard the door close. She stood there, hands behind her back and her eyes were focused onto him. It was bound to happen eventually, the law of the US catching up to her.

He pulled from his jacket a Beretta 9mm equipped with a silencer and started to point it at her. She knew immediately that it was not the US law this man represented but someone else. Her lightening reflexes were far superior then that of the man's. Her knife slammed into his lower chest with a dull thud. The man hunched over from the impact. She was moving right after the throw, not giving him any time to recover. He did recover though and tried to shoot her. She fell into a roll under his aim as a few rounds went off. They were far from their mark as she came up within the man's reach.

Batting the gun to the side with her right arm, she reversed her momentum and stepped into the man. Her elbow connected with the man's jaw and he bent over in a heap. Using her left hand, she grabbed the man by the collar and pulled him towards her. Her knee went up into the man's gut and he gasped for breath. She heard the sound of the gun dropping to the ground and she knew that he was done. Grabbing the back of his hair, she yanked his face up. The man groaned as she clutched the knife in his abdomen. She kicked his hand away from the knife and picked up his gun then knelt beside the man.

She put the gun in the waist of her pants and moved her hand down to the knife handle.

"Who are you, and what do you want with me?" She demanded.

"Ahh… fuck you bitch…." He stated through gritted teeth. She pushed the knife in.

"Ah… I was part.. of… ahh…" the man raspy voice screeched. "You… killed my… ahh… friends."

"Where are the others? I know you are not alone…" She commanded, the knife sliding deeper in.

"Ah… shit…" he protested. "There is just one other…. "He confessed. The revelation was not for her benefit. His hand was on the transmitter he wore and he'd been broadcasting their conversation.

"Where…" Amelie prompted.

The smile on his face was enough to know that the man he had contacted on the radio showed up. He had to be behind her, there was no other place for him to be. She slowly pulled the man up to his feet. She wanted to be up and ready for anything. She watched his eyes and they betrayed him. She spun the man around with her as she reached for the pistol in her waist. She beaded the man standing before her… then froze.

* * *

Trystine shook with fear and she didn't know what was going on. She was crying and wanted to run to Amelie. However, the man holding her wouldn't allow it. Amelie steadied herself trying to judge the reflexes of the man that had a gun to her beloved Trystine.

"You shoot me and the last thing I will do is take another life that you love." The man protested.

"Why did you kill my parents?" she asked. The man in her arms was squirming from weakness and she said, "He is dying"

"We all die Ms. Delauney It's just a matter of how and when." The man countered.

Amelie understood the situation and she knew that this was the end of her, as soon as the man she held died, she would have no way to escape. She looked into the eyes of Trystine and silently whispered a sweet apology. Trystine seemed to have understood and smiled in response.

"What do you propose then?" Amelie flatly asked.

"You die as soon as he does… it's that simple. I go on my merry way back to the US and forget all about you." He said in confidence.

Tears started to form in her eyes then, and Amelie didn't even bother to wipe them away. All that she had loved, all that she wanted, was denied and taken from her. Moreover, she didn't even know why.

"I just want to know one thing… Why my parents?" she sobbed the question.

"You never found out did you?" he questioned back. "Your father had something my boss wanted, he would not sell it to us, and so we tried to steal it." He went on.

"You father's invention jeopardized our government's security." He stated. "He was being unreasonable so we had to fix that."

"So you killed him, and my mother? Why did she have to die and not me?" Amelie asked.

"Your father, yes, he died because he wouldn't give up the secrets that he invented. However, your mother was another story. The two men that raped her were later killed by me when I found out about it." He offered.

"As for you…" he added, "well you turned out to be quite the devil of a killer… I would have never suspected that you were capable of accomplishing what you did."

Amelie started at him hard, thinking of a way to save Trystine. She was grasping for anything that she might find useful. It was a narrow alley and she was running out of time, and options. "I am glad to have disappointed you then."

"A pity you must die." He finished.

Amelie had been silently battling within herself on wanting to kill this man. She hesitated because of Trystine; she didn't want anything to happen to her. When he had mentioned to her *'a devil of a killer'*, she thought about it and decided that he would die today. Even if she, herself died too, she would die knowing that her parents killer's were dead also.

"So where is it?" he asked.

She realized, he must have been talking about my father's notes. He still wanted the work her father did. How interesting. It was time for him to die she decided then. The man in her clutches started to drift away and she knew that he would be dead in the next few seconds. She raised her gun. It seemed like watching movement in water as the gun leveled. He was already aiming at her when she pulled the trigger. He'd gotten his shot off first and his aim was good. She was hit in the shoulder. For the first time in her life, Amelie truly felt pain. It was not from the wound, but from the thought that she would never see Trystine again. Her aim however was better and she hit him square in the forehead.

He fell to the ground and the man in her arms fell at the same time. She stood there for a while holding the pistol at the fallen man. Trystine screamed and Amelie dropped to one knee. Trystine rushed into her arms and held her tight. The gun fell from her hand and Amelie rested her head on the shoulder of her little sister. The blood was slowly coming out of her and it was staining her shirt.

"I love you Tryst." She whispered.

Trystine cried and she held on tight as Amelie's form slumped to the ground. There was more blood and all she could think about was the time her and Trystine had slept together, cuddling all the while. The only time she'd ever found peace in her dreams was when Trystine was with her. She smiled at that and was happy that Trystine was there all those nights and the days they had spent in the fields behind her house.

She was getting cold now and she felt tired. She knew it would be all over in a matter of a few moments and all she wanted was to have Trystine with her. She never knew if Trystine stayed by her side that evening or not, she passed out long before then.

* * *

He was doing his everyday chores when he had heard the screams. They were a high-pitched type of scream that seemed to make his Dalmatian whine. He rushed to the window to find in the ally below a little girl holding onto a young woman. There was blood all over her shirt and there were two dead men in the alley.

He rushed down the stairs while his dog followed. He grabbed blankets and some alcohol along the way. He was an animal vet so he had all the necessary things needed to render aid. There was little time.

He burst out into the ally and moved to the form on the ground. The dog came out after him and started to sniff the girl clutching the women. She had a weak pulse and he knew that if he didn't close the wound, she would die. He brought her and the little girl into his house and called for paramedics.

Epilogue

It has been two weeks since that fateful day. Trystine missed her friend dearly and longed to see her. The events that took place in the market didn't really make much sense to her. The kind man that tried to save her explained some things to her about good and evil. It appeared to her that Amelie was the evil one at first, but when she had learned that Amelie was protecting her, she found a new sense of respect for the friend she look to as a mom.

Trystine stayed at Amelie's home day in and day out tending to the chores that needed to be done. She'd hoped that Amelie would come home, but she never did. It hurt her so much and more often than not, she stayed up late at night crying and holding Amelie's teddy bear.

One day, Trystine decided to try to clean out that dirty basement she had found three weeks earlier. While snooping through some of the boxes, Trystine found a rather thick notebook inside a footlocker. There was another box inside that but it had a combination lock on it. Being a little curious of sorts, Trystine read the notebook and she didn't really understand what she was reading but what she did notice was that the pages bore some sort of mathematical formulas.

Some of the pages contained diagrams and drawings. It looked scientific and she wondered if this was what that bad man was talking to Amelie about that day. Trystine was a bright girl and she knew when something was important. She gingerly gathered the contents of the footlocker and cleaned everything inside. She organized the papers and notebooks based on the numbers on the cover. The she moved the footlocker to a cubby in the corner of the basement.

Her young eyes darted about looking for something that she could use to cover the old dusty trunk. Her eyes settled on a thick wool blanket that was draped over a rocking chair. She grabbed the blanket and flung it out so that it would settle on the trunk with ease. Satisfied with her work she continued on cleaning the rest of the basement.

She spotted another box with some binders in it. She picked them up and wiped off the dust and spider webs. Opening them, she found them to be photo albums. They were photos of Amelie's family. She was looking through them and seeing that Amelie did have a happy child hood. There weren't many photos in the book; in fact, it was half-empty. She traced Amelie's childhood through the years from her birth in Corsica. To her seventh birthday on the farm, that Amelie now owned.

She looked through them and began to feel sorrow for her friend. Trystine was thirteen now and she was moving into womanhood. A lot was changing for her and her loneliness for Amelie was compounding all of her emotions. The pain that crept up on her at night came back ten fold, and Trystine buckled over and started to sob uncontrollably. She clutched the binder in her arms and sat there crying for hours. She kept thinking how she missed her dear friend. Tryst kept praying to god that she'd find the peace that haunted her friend.

That day slipped into night and soon night disappeared into the dreamy sleep that Trystine often experienced. Her slumber was dressed with recent memories of Amelie and their time together. There was no doubt that Trystine loved Amelie and her dream compounded those feelings while she was awake. Trystine had grown up on the ruthless streets of Marseille and Beuvron-en-Auge and when she had met Amelie on the road, Trystine started to develop a strong sense of a maternal bond with the mysterious woman.

The next morning found Trystine with a bit if the sun's rays peeking through the stormy rain clouds outside. Her spirits where down from the previous night's dreams and Trystine was hoping that the day would go better. She still waited, as she did every morning, for a phone call or for Amelie to open the door. As the clock on the wall tracked time, Trystine slowly started realize that none of this would happen. She was beginning to accept the truth.

A knock on the door startled her from her thoughts and Trystine almost burst through the door but she remembered what Amelie had said all the time when they would get company.

Never open a door unless you are sure you know who is on the other side.

She remembered, in fact, almost lived by that rule. Amelie was a good mentor and she always looked out for Trystine. She missed her friend with each passing moment. Her excitement had almost gotten the best of her though.

All of it was hard on the girl so when she was visited by the man she knew as Dave, the one who came to the rescue of her and her dear friend, she was somewhat happy. He'd come to take her to the hospital, the place where he had taken Amelie for care. She was excited that maybe Amelie was ok and wanted so badly to see her again.

They arrived at the hospital that afternoon and the place was full of sick people. Dave had insisted that Trystine be allowed to come with them during visiting hours. His reasoning was that Amelie was Trystine's guardian. At first, the nurse hesitated but then the look on Tryst's face convinced her that there was no harm in allowing the girl to come along.

The door opened and Trystine immediately ran in searching for her maternal friend. There she was. Trystine couldn't contain herself and allowed a bright big smile creep across her face. She ran to Amelie proclaiming her love for the wounded woman.

"Amelie, I've missed you so much!" She declared. Amelie just smiled at her and touched her cheek.

The two of them held each other for a long moment and Dave thought he would begin to cry.

"I want you to be my mommy? Will you take care of me and can we be a family?" Trystine said gingerly.

Amelie gently pulled her head forward and kissed Trystine on the top of her head. She starred at the girl for a long moment looking into her bright green eyes.

"You will always be my little one. Tryst you mean the world to me."

Amelie looked at Dave and he just smiled at the scene before him. It made him feel good that these two could be reunited. She reached out to him offering her hand. He grasped it firmly and she returned the sincerity.

Dave stood there for a moment admiring the both of them. Admired them for what they were to each other. Two souls lost in a world of warped and twisted morals, where man betrayed one another for the sake of personal gain. A world where the love of family was over shadowed by personal greed and these two people managed to survive beyond all that and find each other and to create something magical of their own. He let go of her hand then, nodded to her and exited the room.

* * *

Dave left the hospital and drove to the police station. He had an appointment with the inspector over what had happened that day in the village. When the police found out about Dave's background, they immediately offered their support. He didn't like the attention but for the sake of saving the young girl, he'd put up with it.

The local substation was located in Marseille so the trip wasn't long. All the while Dave found himself thinking about Amelie and the little girl. As soon as he was done with this inspector, he would return to the hospital to pick up Trystine. She was a cute girl and would be a heart breaker when she got older, he thought.

The Substation wasn't very busy and parking was easy. Dave exited his car and started walking towards the front entrance when something caught his attention. A group of men in black suits exited the side and boarded an unmarked Mercedes SUV. Usually the police would not allow people to move in and out of certain areas of the compound, so Dave figured that these men were important or something.

He entered the station and looked around, then was escorted to a waiting room and the clerk closed the door behind him. It wasn't too uncomfortable for him, there were magazines on the table to read, a newspaper, the TV was on but the volume was low and there was a coffee machine brewing coffee.

That struck Dave as odd. As far as he knew, the French usually didn't drink your standard coffee. They preferred a certain style of drinks like Lattés and the like. He peered out the window and noticed that someone was walking around his car. Dave started to become a bit aware then and knew that something was amiss with his visit to the substation.

Just then, the door opened and a finely dressed man entered. His hair was black, combed and sleek. His broad shoulders filled out the trench coat that he wore and the cleanly shaven face belied his age. Dave could tell that the man was older than he looked. Just by the texture of his cheeks. His hands were rough and he was starting to form blotches on his skin. He was distinguished and well carried.

"Major Lee, Correct?" the man said in a heavy accent.

"That's me, and you are?" Dave led on.

"I am inspector Devereux. " He stated. "Tell me… what brings you to France?"

"After my retirement, I decided to move to a quiet pocket of the world." Dave said with a smile. "You know, to get away."

"Born here, not much choice" Devereux said a length. "I read your report and was confused on a few points."

"Ah, which sections?" Dave asked.

Devereux began to talk when another man entered to room followed by more men, six in total. The first one bent down and whispered in Devereux's ear and Devereux nodded, stood and left the room.

"Wait? What's going on?" Dave demanded.

"I'm sorry Mr. Lee, but I will be handling the case from this point forward" The man paused.

"Who are…," Dave started.

"That is not important. What is important is that Amelie is watched over." He interrupted. "You see, she is of interest to the Department of the Interior and we need someone that has no affiliation with France or the Department to keep an eye on her."

"Wait, you mean you want me to spy on her for you?" Dave said quizzically. This was bad, he thought. For some reason these people high up had Amelie's health in their best interests. This is getting more and more interesting by the minute.

"So she is important to you?" He poked.

"Yes, but she doesn't know it, and you are not going to tell her either." The Commandant said. "You see, this is all about something that her father possessed, yet he was killed years ago in a

CIA sting. We have reason to believe that they are here again looking to finish what they started" the man explained. "The items were never recovered. Either she knows where they are or she doesn't know she has them. It will be your job to ensure her safety incase they try again."

"Absolutely not" Dave stated.

"On the contrary, you will… or the girl goes to prison in an American facility and the little girl will go back to the orphanage she escaped from."

"You do care about her don't you?" the man finished.

"From what I understand, you are more than qualified to perform this request, yes?" He offered Dave a prodding glare.

"Yeah… I do" All Dave was thinking about were the moments when the two girls were reunited, the joy that the little one expressed and how he could tell that those two needed one another.

Dave was not an intuitive person but for some strange reason he knew that separating those two would be bad for who ever was responsible.

"What did she do back in the states?" Dave asked.

"Oh she killed a Mayor and a few cops, left a blood trail that led nowhere as far as the FBI was concerned." The man was fiddling with his pen. "In exchange for this, she will be given a pardon for the death of the men she killed at the market and I'll have my people give a plausible story to your government as to what happened."

"Ok, I'll look out for her until you say otherwise" Dave measured the words carefully. He didn't want to get caught up in the middle of an international scandal.

"Good, then it is done." The man turned to one of the others and nodded.

"You will be compensated for your time, no doubt. I'll have an agent stop by your manor with the paperwork required for your employment. If you don't have any questions, I am sure she will be able to answer any that might arise then." The Commandant got up.

"This is of the utmost importance and keeping her safe until we can approach her on the matter is your primary objective." They exited the room and left Dave there to think about the situation.

Dave didn't know what to think. He had seen the aftermath of some fight between her and a few dead bodies. He had no idea that she was capable of killing a public official, let alone getting out of the country unscathed. Well not entirely…, those men found her and they weren't Interpol. So that led him to believe that they were company men or mercenaries. More like company men. Then why hasn't he seen Interpol poking around looking for answers? That would mean that either they were working unsanctioned. More than likely, they were mercs and Dave didn't worry about the lot of that kind.

He'd dealt with a few good mercs in his own time.

Walking out to his car seemed like a dream, he didn't even remember walking or listening to the sounds of traffic horns. All he could think about where the possible dangers that he would have to face if things were to become shaky.

Dave's thoughts lingered on the fact that he knew almost nothing about this girl. She was beautiful and at the same time, possessed an aura of danger and intrigue. He didn't know what to think about all that had unfolded in the past few weeks. He'd just been commissioned by the French government to ensure the safety of Amelie. What could be so important about the items she had in her possession?

The weight of his situation was getting heavy and he felt that people might die. Dave's background gave him the skills necessary to perform this request. This would be nothing compared to the missions he'd been on with his SOCOM unit in the teams.

He would have to break out his equipment and make a few calls back to the states but he was getting paid for a job that would help him retire earlier than planned and he'd get a chance to learn more about her and what she possessed.

Still though, he knew that the French would monitor him as well, after all he was American. The operation was freelanced and he knew that the anonymity the French needed would be through him. Dave would get a chance at getting to know Amelie better and possibly the mystery that surrounded her.

* * *

What Dave didn't know was that a not so well known secret organization was vying to obtain the technology for purposes of its own. That Amelie was expendable once the technology was recovered. Dave didn't know that he unwillingly helped this organization to move a plot forward that would bring the international Intelligence community to its knees.

END

About the author

Quentin Daschel Lee grew up in Las Vegas and originally wanted to become a police officer. Unfortunate events caused him to reconsider his future. Quentin started to explore his artistic ability to tell stories soon after. He began writing fictional stories on the internet and quickly became a favorite among his peers. His dream is to become a screenwriter and his books reflect the movies he wishes to make.

Quentin is currently working on the adaptation to this novel and is expected to finish by the summer of 2007.

www.ingramcontent.com/pod-product-compliance
Lightning Source LLC
LaVergne TN
LVHW090953080826
845145LV00003B/997

* 9 7 8 0 9 7 8 9 0 0 7 0 0 *